'89 WALLS

by Katie Pierson

Paperback ISBN: 978-1-940014-55-5
E-book ISBN: 978-1-940014-62-3
Library of Congress Control Number: 2015940936

Cover design by Jessie Sayward Bright
Page layout and design by Emily Shaffer Rodvold at Lift Creative
Typeset in Adobe Garamond Pro.

Printed in the United States of America
Second printing: 2015
17 16 15 14 13   5 4 3 2

Wise Ink Creative Publishing
Minneapolis, MN
612-200-0983, www.wiseinkpub.com

To order, visit www.itascabooks.com or call 1-800-901-3480. Reseller discounts available. For orders other than by individual consumers, the author grants a discount on the purchase of 10 or more copies for special markets or premium use (such as nonprofit donor gifts). For further details or to order, visit www.katiepierson.net.

"'Of course it means you are going away from us for good,' she said with a sigh. 'But that don't mean I'll lose you. Look at my papa here; he's been dead all these years, and yet he is more real to me than almost anybody else. He never goes out of my life. I talk to him and consult him all the time. The older I grow, the better I know him and the more I understand him.'"

—*My Ántonia* by Willa Cather

With abiding love and respect for my father,
David C. Pierson, 1935–1989.

PROLOGUE

Seth wanted to break up with Quinn. But for that to make sense, she'd at least have to know his name.

The paralyzing personal hell of committing to a one-way relationship started on the first day of tenth grade. He'd dropped his pencil on the floor and leaned out of his seat to grab it. This quiet, pretty, dark-haired girl sitting in front of him reached back for it at the same time. Her long hair hid her face, but as she passed him the eraserless no. 2 (that he regretted chewing on ten seconds ago), her warm fingertips brushed his palm.

"Thanks," he whispered to her back.

She turned around and smiled at him like this whole thing was normal. She whispered, "You're welcome."

That was it. All she'd done was hand him his pencil.

CHAPTER 1
GLASNOST

Quinn stood in the tiled foyer of her silent house, breathing in the soothing smell of dusting spray that the cleaning lady left behind. She tossed her backpack and jean jacket onto a dining room chair and headed for the sunlit kitchen. Bypassing the colander of green grapes by the sink, she picked through the snack bowl and settled on a half sleeve of crackers. She found a block of cheddar in the fridge. She stood at the butcher block, slicing the cheese and making tiny sandwiches.

After her snack, she gripped the oiled banister and took the stairs two at a time. At the top, she could practically taste the smell of clean laundry. She went to claim her stack. Her mom did the folding while returning phone calls but drew the line at putting the clothes back in their drawers.

"I'm not your maid," Quinn had heard her say, ad nauseam.

Quinn pushed herself up onto the washing machine's smooth surface and dialed the number for her sister, Sarah. As the phone rang, she wrapped the phone's coiled cord around her forearm, poking white dots onto her skin between the black rings of stretchy plastic. She'd learned to avoid getting banished to the living room phone by unwrapping the cord slowly; if she unwrapped it too fast, she'd leave an ugly kink in the spiral. Her mom hated it when she did that.

"Hello?" Sarah said.

"It's me," said Quinn. "I was wondering if you could come over for a food fight."

"How about a midnight run to the U-Stop? I could go for a blue raspberry slush."

"I'd kill right now for some sour cream and cheddar potato chips. Mom's starving us out with grainy wholesome goodness."

Sarah had moved to New York two years ago. The bathroom the two of them once shared seemed stark without Sarah's sweaty leotards wadded in the corners. She had attended a local community college for four months before dropping out to start a dance career. She probably still got an allowance. Quinn missed her, but in a twisty, relieved sort of way. The guilty weight of being the successful daughter, the one without dyslexia (and possibly even her dad's favorite) hadn't lifted until Sarah had sailed out the door.

"Jason and I started having sex," Quinn said.

"What? Why?"

"I don't know. Why does anyone have sex? I couldn't come up with a good reason to keep saying no. We've been together since November."

"Hitting the five-month mark doesn't sound like a good reason to say yes."

Quinn could hear Sarah frowning. "I'm not saying we're not in love or anything. We're in lust."

"So the sex is good then?"

"Good?"

"God, Quinn, can you hear yourself? Don't do it. You're not ready."

Usually, Sarah could boost Quinn's confidence with her signature blasts of praise and loyalty. When Quinn had fretted about getting into colleges, Sarah had shaken her head at her like Quinn was smoking crack. "Of course you'll get in," she'd said. End of discussion. Sarah also knew things about guys. She split them into two essential groups—princes and toads—usually within thirty seconds of meeting them.

"I already did it," Quinn said. "That horse is out of the gate, so to speak. Besides, what do you mean *good*?"

"Fun. Hot. Cuddly. Thrilling. Is that what it's like?"

They'd only done it a few times. But no, it wasn't. Jason was a great kisser, or used to be back when they did a lot of kissing. But kissing had dropped down on the priority list. And the actual sex part—once the novelty factor wore off—seemed like more trouble and mess than it was worth.

"I guess Jason thinks it is."

"He's still hot, huh?"

"Totally."

The first time Quinn met Jason, she and her friend Ilene had competed against him and another guy in a tournament. Quinn and Ilene could tell that they'd lost that round before the judge even posted her results.

"That was a fucking train wreck," Ilene said, shaking her head.

Quinn smiled. She used to be intimidated by her new debate partner's self-contained, perfectionist brilliance. Now, when Ilene let fly with one of her sarcastic profanity bombs, it felt like insider intel on their real friendship.

Jason and his partner apparently also knew that they'd won the round. They did a quiet high five.

Quinn shoved her files into her briefcase, then sat back in her chair, trying not to pout on the outside.

Jason crossed the room. He held out his palms in silent repentance. His wry smile tried to apologize for his disarming, Indian gorgeousness, but Quinn ignored him. Having been dumped publicly a few weeks earlier by Chris, a fast-talking brainiac from Omaha, Quinn was done with debate guys. They were fun to sneak a cigarette with between rounds, but deep down, they were socially retarded and had hearts of stone.

But Jason sat right on her desk. This made him harder to ignore. Then he took the fountain pen she was twirling between her fingers and tossed it in the air. As Quinn stood and caught it, she accidentally-on-purpose shoved him off the desk. He just barely managed to regain his footing. Widening his eyes but not taking them off hers, he laughed. Then he held out his hand.

"I'm Jason Singh."

She raised an eyebrow and suppressed her smile as long as she could, like she hadn't already made up her mind.

"Quinn Ganey."

She'd expected her parents to mention the race thing, but her dad only mused that some of the best scientists in the world were Asians. (Quinn learned later that Mrs. Singh was a hematologist.)

Her father had offered a similar, admiring non sequitur when Quinn broke up with Evan Schwartz in ninth grade, something about the Jews one day taking over the world.

"Still, I don't care how beautiful he is," Sarah said now. "You should hold out for good sex."

"I can't suddenly change my mind."

"Why not? Is there an official sex rulebook? Go back to oral."

"He doesn't like it." Quinn heard silence on the other end of the line.

"I don't understand."

"I mean he only likes it when I do it. Not the other way around."

Sarah snorted. "That's pathetic, Quinn. What are you, a battered wife or something? I say that, of course, in the nicest, most loving possible way."

"And yet I take that as a messed-up, mixed message, Sarah. And I mean that in the most mind-your-own-business possible way."

"Hey, you're the one who called me." Sarah had a point there. "Just wait. For now, you should stick to having sex with yourself."

"Ew," Quinn whined.

"Oh, please. Everyone does it, including you. " That was another fair point.

After hanging up with Sarah, Quinn took her stack of clean clothes to her room. She heaped it on her desk chair and closed the heavy door. Her bedroom was a time capsule from her misguided ninth-grade mauve phase. Only her new Macintosh II and printer, with its trail of continuous-feed paper, offered a clue that a near-adult lived here. Flopping on her bed, Quinn kicked off her pointy flats. She rubbed the beginnings of another blister. Wearing socks with flats only made sense if you didn't have a problem with social death.

Her room overlooked the front yard. Or it would until the Japanese maple leafed out and blocked her view. In the summer, she didn't even pull her curtains. Last night, the moon had hovered full and low between the budding branches. She'd heaved open the window next to her bed. She could smell that her dad had been raking. Eyes closed, she'd breathed in the perfume of damp dirt shedding its winter layers of leaf mulch. It made her want to do some shedding of her own, to rip off a Band-Aid or cut her hair or do something shocking to her sweet, precious wallpaper.

Prince, Madonna, and Duran Duran glowered out at her from their posters on the wall as if they too chafed under their oppressively ninth-grade surroundings. Quinn pressed on one of the puffy square baffles on her mauve bedspread. When she slid her fingers over to the next one, she snagged a fresh hangnail on a loop of clear thread.

She sighed. Last night, Jason had asked her to his prom. He wanted to go with his squirrely pot-smoking friends and their dates—then rent a hotel room. Quinn thought about her conversation with Sarah. If she and Jason rented a hotel room, would they have good sex or just sex? And how the hell would she know the difference? She sighed again and started her homework.

The next afternoon, Quinn stood at her locker and tucked in the white cotton strap of her bra. It had sneaked beyond the boundaries of her sleeveless sundress and bugged her all day. She liked how the dial on her locker's padlock kind of twirled itself, how the lock released with a pleasing "thunk." She smoothed her hair behind her ears.

Terrence—whom she'd known since kindergarten—half strutted, half bounced to his locker on Quinn's right. He nodded a greeting down to her but directed his opening volley over her head to the guy opening the locker on her left.

"Yo, man, this girl was *all over* me," he said. "I'm telling her, 'This is my little brother's recital, a'right?'" He primped his oiled curls with one hand and spun his lock with the other.

The dim fluorescent lighting in the second-floor hallway made the other guy's red hair look even redder. He rolled his eyes at Terrence but said nothing. His asymmetrical flop hairdo screamed 1986. This was 1989.

Quinn returned Terrence's smile, yawning as she opened her locker. It was April of her senior year; at this point, she was a tolerant but bored bystander in this mildly amusing testosterone war. Terrence caught his cardboard breakdancing mat as it sprung out of his locker. Quinn knelt on the marble floor and pried a notebook from the bottom shelf of hers. The lock caught with a bump of her hip as she stood up. She dodged her way through the hallway traffic.

The stalls, floor tiles, and walls of the girls' room rocked the same relentless hue of hospital green, inflicting a universally un-flattering glare on all who entered. Quinn headed for a toilet. She'd drunk a huge Coke with lunch.

From her stall, Quinn heard her best friend, Trish, demand of her from the sinks, "Do I *look* like someone who does crepe paper?"

They met here every day at the same time. Quinn could picture Trish standing with one hand on her narrow hip. The other would be raised as if to say, "What?" She was bitching about her latest run-in with the office secretary/prom-committee advisor. The secretary was outflanked; she just didn't know it yet.

Trish and Quinn's mutual, total failure to do a flexed-arm hang for the Presidential Physical Fitness Test had sealed their friendship in seventh grade. Trish had observed out loud that only stupid people hung from a metal bar on purpose. This was a revelation to Quinn. And unlike Quinn, Trish had been tested for real. Trish's dad had just moved out. Her family-minus-one was renting what would become a series of apartments in a sun-baked complex near Highway 2. Sooner or later the neighbors always complained about the kid noise. Then Trish and her mom would carry their stuff down two floors or over one building.

Quinn had spent her junior high years at track meets with her older sister and parents and taking private piano lessons. Trish, meanwhile, had been supervising her little brothers' homework and making scrambled eggs for dinner. Quinn remembered Trish's mom creeping around the apartment in her sweatpants after work, looking like a weepy volunteer for an experiment in sleep deprivation.

In ninth grade, though, Trish's mom married a real estate developer. He moved the family into a big new house with pillars. Now that Trish had landed the part she'd always meant to play, she acted it out daily in full costume. Once, Quinn teased her about her conversion to the church of Ralph Lauren. Trish had put her fingers in her ears like the manic television icon, Pee-wee Herman: "La, la, la! I can't hear you!" The real Trish was still there, though. She was still flip, still funny, still the unflappable arbiter of cool. Sometimes Trish's enveloping audacity was the only thing that kept Quinn from evaporating into thin air.

As Trish addressed the perma-wedgie situation caused by her trendy new jeans, Quinn washed her hands with the dispenser's last few grains of powdered soap. She frowned. How could Trish look self-possessed even with her forearms down the back of her pants? The problem with being friends with audacious people was that it made you see your own fraudulence more clearly.

She faced her reflection as she rinsed off the non-suds left by the industrial soap. "A quiet beauty," her dad called her. She'd rather be a loud one. Her breasts were okay, but who would know besides Jason? Her parents, especially her dad, didn't let her wear anything tight or revealing. Quinn's fine brown hair refused to be styled, so she wore it parted on the side. It bored her to even think about it. Trish caught her eye and, as usual, read her mind.

"If you spent some of your humongous allowance on funner clothes, you wouldn't mind having boring hair."

Quinn made a face at her. Trish knew why Quinn saved her spending money: her parents expected her to pay for a full semester plus books at George Washington University next year.

"Funner's not a word," Quinn said, probing a subterranean zit. The light-blue eyes that looked back from the mirror were her father's and a million other Irish family members'. They smiled even when her mouth didn't. They also kept a polite distance; even with nice breasts, no one would ever mistake her for a cheerleader.

CHAPTER 2
COVERT INTELLIGENCE

A pparently, Mr. Levine had been messing with the blinds again; three of them were hanging at steep angles. The state of the blinds, though, Quinn noted, was incidental to the general chaos of the classroom itself. Dusty books seemed to slouch in their sagging bookcases, and they teetered in stacks on top. Towers of papers, dirty coffee cups, and floppy file folders carpeted Mr. Levine's desk. A healthy-looking spider plant scattered its lime-green shoots over the whole mess. From a ceiling tile overhead, President Kennedy ordered her not to ask what her country could do for her, but what she could do for her country.

"It looks like the Cold War may be thawing out," Mr. Levine announced to the class. He punched a fist in the air like he'd pulled this off himself. A few people laughed. "If this turns out to be the end of the world as we know it, I'll have to rewrite my whole curriculum."

Mr. Levine was known for his gloves-off class discussions and for not giving tests, both of which attracted college-bound seniors like Quinn to his U.S. foreign relations class. He was kind of handsome for a guy in his forties. He wore his curly light-brown hair cut short and looked like he worked out. Rumor had it that he went out with the new English teacher with the miniskirts.

"Seriously," Mr. Levine said. "You and I are living through one of the strangest moments in history. Soviet communism is on the run. American democracy and capitalism are winning. We know it. Gorbachev knows it. And here's the score: five decades of communism have produced three hundred million Soviets who have no incentive to get out of bed unless they want to stand in line all day for canned cabbage."

He pointed to the chalkboard where he'd copied a quote from President Reagan's speech in Berlin two years ago: "General Secretary Gorbachev, if you seek peace, if you seek prosperity for the Soviet Union and Eastern Europe, if you seek liberalization, come here to this gate. Mr. Gorbachev, open this gate. Mr. Gorbachev, tear down this wall!"

Quinn had kept up with the newspaper lately since it was one of the few basic requirements of this class. The headlines had shouted for months about the Soviets trying to keep their economy from imploding. Still, the end of the Cold War was a lot to absorb in a seventh-period class on a Tuesday. The forty-four-year nuclear arms race between the United States and the Soviet Union—and the probability of everyone getting blown to smithereens in World War III—had been the fundamental political fact of her existence. It felt surreal, like someone had spliced a Disney cartoon onto the end of a James Bond movie.

Quinn looked around. Her own blank expression wasn't the only one. Mr. Levine smiled. Hopping off the desk, he scooped some Jolly Rancher candies out of his top drawer and put them in his pocket. He wove his fingers together and cracked his knuckles over his head in one sickening crunch.

"Here's what we're going to do. We're going to spend the next two months deciding what our new president, George H. W. Bush, should do with this Cold War victory. Does America take a break after fifty years on the world's stage? Or do we have a mandate to herd the world toward democracy and capitalism?"

Her Republican dad, Quinn knew, would state a theory or quote Montesquieu or some other dead text that he read for fun. He'd drone on about the last eight thrilling years of trickle-down Reaganomics. Sometimes, Quinn liked to describe Mr. Levine's classroom discussions to her dad. As fun as it was to bait him, though, she did it mostly to figure out the right answers. Politics didn't affect her much personally, but she wasn't stupid: she knew she only heard one side of any issue at the dinner table. Her dad's friendly teasing and carefully reasoned opinions usually made her agree with him in the end, but she still wanted to get the whole story.

Quinn raised her hand. She had learned how to dodge the Socratic bullet of being called on randomly in this class. Mr. Levine bowed his head in her direction.

"Senator Ganey, you have the floor."

"I think it's a mandate," she said. Her face got hot. Two years on the varsity debate team and she still turned red every single time she spoke in public. "If the United States stopped leading now, it would be like we'd fought the Cold War for nothing."

Mr. Levine sat on the teeny edge of empty real estate on his messy desk. "What's our goal then? Are we spreading democracy? Making the world safe for capitalism?"

Quinn thought for a second, twisting the pearl stud in her earlobe. "Both," she said. "I mean, we're winning because we're right."

She heard a disgusted groan from the other side of the room and looked over. Seth Burton was staring right at her with a you've-got-to-be-kidding expression on his face. She scowled back at him. If he was so brilliant, why didn't he speak up? She stared him down until he looked away. Asshole. Mr. Levine tossed Quinn a Jolly Rancher. She caught it.

She'd felt sorry for Seth when she'd first met him years ago; he obviously came from a poor family. He seemed chronically stressed out. Until she shared Mr. Levine's class with him, though, she'd never even heard him speak in complete sentences, let alone smart ones. Now that she clashed almost daily with his cynical intelligence and hostility toward the world, however, he annoyed the hell out of her. And sometimes, like now, he made her feel like the most frivolous, spoiled person on earth. She quit twisting her pearl.

Mr. Levine stopped in front of the blackboard. Drew raised his hand and started talking.

"I agree with Quinn," Drew said. "Who else will spread democracy if we don't? I mean, what's the point of becoming the best player on the team if you stay on the bench?" Drew wasn't a bad guy, but he liked the sound of his own voice. He also managed to wedge sports metaphors into every conversation. Mr. Levine winged him a Jolly Rancher. Drew caught it one-handed.

Quinn sneaked another glance at Seth, who was now rolling his eyes. Drew must have noticed, too.

"Dude, do you have something to say to me?" he asked Seth.

Seth winced as though he were in pain. Even his jeans looked defeated, like they'd gone too long between washes. But he didn't even blink when he turned to face Drew. "Yeah, actually, I do," he said. "I agree that we should help other democracies. But we should do it on their terms. We say all the time that we're fighting for freedom when we're actually fighting for capitalism."

"Prove it," Drew sneered. He was acting like a jerk.

"Guatemala, Chile, Nicaragua."

Drew looked to Mr. Levine for clarification.

"Yes," Mr. Levine said slowly. "Seth reminds us that being 'winners' of the Cold War doesn't mean we're the squeaky clean good guys. In Latin America, the U.S. has made kind of a habit of kicking out democratically elected socialists. We like to prop up military governments instead that play nice with American capitalists. Our reasoning is something like, 'Well, they're murdering dictators, but at least they're not communists.'"

Quinn's neck hair bristled. "But isn't that true?" she asked. "Isn't it better in the long run if we roll back communism?"

"It depends on who you ask," Seth said grimly, looking straight at her. "Our government would say yes. But the people who elected their own leaders and then watched us replace them with military thugs? They'd probably say no."

Seth seemed unaware that his snide, save-the-world lectures

were completely pretentious. It was okay with her if people criticized the government; it was a free country. But it went up her butt a mile that left-wingers—like him and her friends on the school paper, with their moth-eaten vintage clothes and their ugly Birkenstock sandals—seemed to get off on America's mistakes. She broke his gaze.

Fierce-looking Michelle raised her hand. Quinn didn't understand the whole Goth girl thing: and her own parents would kill her if she triple pierced her ears. Quinn respected Michelle, though; she'd gotten sent home last semester for protesting douche commercials. She'd worn (and refused to take off) a button that said, "The Vagina Is a Self-Cleaning Organ."

"I don't get it," Michelle asked. "Why would a military government be friendlier to capitalism than communists would?"

Mr. Levine showed her a green candy before putting both hands behind his back. When Michelle pointed at his right hand, he tossed it to her.

"In a nutshell," he said, "people who survive dictators, colonialism, and civil wars that kill their families and starve their children are really, really pissed off."

Quinn had grasped early on that Mr. Levine was a liberal, but she didn't mind; he didn't act like a stereotypical Democrat. Unlike some of her friends who lobbed their lefty views like self-evident truths, Mr. Levine dealt in facts. Before taking this class, though, Quinn had never heard a teacher use the expression "pissed off."

"Unstable countries make poor markets for American capitalists," he went on, pacing the front of the room. "So once in a while, America goes ahead and creates 'stability' on its own terms." He stopped pacing. "Capisce?" he asked, holding his right thumb and fingers together like Marlon Brando in *The Godfather*. Most of the class signaled yes.

"Good discussion, folks," said Mr. Levine. The sound of him rubbing his dry palms together made Quinn cringe. "But I want to get back to Drew's point. What would have happened after World War II—another new day in American history—if the United States had stayed on the bench? Has anyone heard of the Marshall Plan?"

"We rebuilt Europe," Ilene said. She sat in the desk next to Quinn's. Quinn gave her the eye contact version of a high five. Mr. Levine walked over and placed a candy on Ilene's pencil tray.

"Yes. We'd led the Allies to victory and kept leading. It was a good thing for everyone, including us. But does 'winning' the Cold War put us in the same position? Are we heroes again now, or are we simply the last ones standing?"

Seth spoke up. "I think we're just the last ones standing. We haven't perfected democracy or anything. It's like we've been saying for fifty years, 'Yeah, kids are starving in America, but at least we're not brutal communists.'"

Mr. Levine nodded at Seth. "Maybe having a reliable enemy like the Soviet Union lets us off easy?" Mr. Levine asked.

This was true, Quinn realized with kind of a jolt. It made her want to question her dad about his tidy theories. Like if Reagan had been such a plain-spoken genius, why did some people still go hungry? She'd probably keep these doubts to herself, though. She'd learned from bruising experience that if she challenged her dad without first chasing down every statistic about welfare queens, he'd tease her about her idealism and the emotional flaws in her logic. It was easier to keep quiet than to walk away with her self-respect all crumpled around the edges.

"Any hands?" asked Mr. Levine. He raised his own, showing a belt-level gap in his oxford cloth shirt where it was missing a button.

Quinn looked over at Seth again. He was doodling. Sometimes he wore a stubbly goatee. Today, though, his tan cheeks were smooth. Quinn looked out the window. The bright April sunshine elbowed its way into the room in uneven blocks between the metal shafts of the blinds.

"What do you think, folks?" Mr. Levine asked. "Should we lead the rest of the world toward democracy and capitalism? Will America use this pause in hostilities to fix what's broken in our own backyard? Will we conjure up a new enemy to spare ourselves the icky feeling of self-reflection?" Total silence. "Shoot. I was hoping you guys knew the answers 'cause I sure don't."

Mr. Levine had ten seconds before the bell rang.

"We're living through an incredibly weird political moment, folks. The whole world is waiting for us to decide who we are."

As Quinn packed up her stuff, Seth walked by her row of desks. She looked up. She could tell he noticed her watching him. But he avoided eye contact, confirming that the smartest guy in the class thought she was a total moron. Not that she cared.

CHAPTER 3
STRATEGIC DEFENSE INITIATIVE

The next day, Seth stood in front of his locker, smelling the gross, sweaty steam oozing out of the locker rooms. He was in an airless, nearly deserted hallway that led to cutting-edge academic classes like pottery and yearbook journalism. This part of the school was a boxy 1970s addition to the much classier main building. From the outside, it looked like it was crouching, like it knew it was an architectural outcast.

As usual, Seth had spent the first six periods of the day waiting for, but dreading, the seventh. He wiped his sweaty hands on his jeans and then traced the outlines of the month-old letter folded inside his pocket. He pulled it out for the millionth time to reread his cramped handwriting: "I've liked you since the beginning of tenth grade. We haven't had any big conversations, but . . ."

Layers of faint thumb smudges had accumulated in the top right corner. They mocked him as he refolded the note and stuffed it back into his pocket. Senior year was almost over. Soon, Seth knew, he'd never see Quinn Ganey again. If he didn't take action, all this unspent . . . whatever . . . would be pointless. It was a matter of diminishing returns, really; hope used to outweigh his fear. Now Seth felt hardly any hope at all and crept around school wanting to hurl eighty percent of the time. The only way to escape this soul-killing purgatory was to put the note in her hand already.

Once, Seth had watched her eat lunch with friends at a big table, listening to her loud laugh ping across the cafeteria. Her straight posture and careful comments in class made her seem sort of dignified, but she had this laugh—this rolling, little-girly giggle—that would explode out of her like pop from a shaken can. Drew, an arrogant jock in her group, catapulted a greasy kernel of canned corn into her hair. Quinn pretended not to notice. But then, when Drew started harassing a new target, she lobbed her entire hamburger across the table, smacking him hard on the side of his face and smearing mustard on his shoulder. Seth had smiled into his peanut butter sandwich. The girl had balls.

At the beginning of sophomore year, he'd observed Quinn hovering around the edges of the popular group before quietly joining their ranks. His self-loathing didn't fully set in, though, until club fair day in the cafeteria, when he saw her sitting with the Young Republicans. Ouch. Leave it to him to fall for someone who was both out of his league and beneath his dignity.

She made friends with everyone, though, not just the people who looked like her or lived in her neighborhood. She'd never been anything but friendly to him. But—and this was weird—she really seemed to think everyone *was* the same, that the whole world had the same chances as she did.

Seth enjoyed watching the vulnerable, tense line show up between her eyebrows when the class discussion clashed with whatever it said in the right-wing handbook. But the views she shared in class made him crazy. This wasn't solely because he thought Republicans were heartless bastards. It was that her outside voice didn't match the person he could see on the inside. Lately, though, her comments had sounded more reflective and real.

Seth slammed the door of his locker. It pinched the callused underside of his thumb and hurt like hell. For almost three years, he'd seen Quinn move through her life as though she expected it to be kind, like someone who had perfect parents who Bubble-Wrapped her in childish curfews and rules meant to keep her from straying. Seth didn't have the time or the energy to stray.

Sometimes—especially when his mom was backsliding—Seth's crush on Quinn congealed into flat-out resentment. He could tell that she'd lived her whole, perfect life in Lincoln, Nebraska. She didn't seem to get it that this town was the kind of place that people only came *from*; nobody except Southeast Asian refugees and university professors came *to* it. And kids like him, uprooted against their will from real cities.

Lincoln had that smug, small-town thing. It got all swelled up over its pioneer history and civic pride. But it ignored what it didn't want to see, such as the weed-choked sidewalks and long blocks of tiny, disintegrating houses in Seth's neighborhood. No wonder his mom had moved them here from Virginia to get a leg up on a landscaping career; he'd never seen a place that needed it more. It's not like his mom loved it, either. She'd told him years ago to please go to college in an interesting city.

She'd smiled. "And invite me to visit."

Resenting Quinn, unfortunately, didn't keep Seth from liking her. Or fantasizing about her; they'd done it a thousand times in his mind.

At the end of the hall, two tiny Vietnamese girls bounced up and down, squealing like rabbits on each impact.

"He asked! I'm going!" Another breathless conversation about senior prom. Perfect. Like he needed another reminder that high school social rituals—stupid or not—didn't include him.

Seth slumped against his dented locker and sucked the sore white ridge on his thumb. The hallway clock gave him two more minutes. His heart drummed against his ribcage as he touched the folded edge of the note in his pocket. He hoisted up his backpack and swiped his hair out of his eyes. He hated any kind of change—probably because he never got to instigate it himself. But suffering the consequences now had to be better than just plain suffering, right?

He decided he'd wait for her outside class. Today. As of now, it had officially become unbearable to carry around an unread love note.

CHAPTER 4
FIRST-STRIKE CAPABILITY

Quinn used the three extra minutes before class that day to turn in her cap-and-gown order form at the office. She made sure no one was looking before skipping down the marble staircase like a little kid. She watched her light-green sundress rise and settle with each bounce. The translucent afternoon sun had managed to warm the foyer by the entrance doors as if spring might actually stick. A tiny breeze jiggled the branches of the narrow pine trees framing the building's entrance. The stretch of blue sky spanning the transom window reassured her, like it was telling her that years of self-conscious high school angst were almost over.

Only her best friend Trish understood how crucial Quinn's façade of success was to the fact of it. As long as she stuck to the script—Take the advanced placement classes. Study. Join the debate team. Perform.—she could hold herself together. She could no more drop the script than let her bones dissolve.

Quinn hated the debate team.

She stomped on the final step. As she rounded the bottom of the stairwell, she saw Seth walking to class from the opposite direction. His dark-blond hair looked like it wanted to cover his eyes but was failing at it. Even looking at him made her feel defensive.

He drew near enough for Quinn to read his T-shirt. A cartoon of Uncle Sam silk-screened in black-and-white on the front said, "Join the army. Travel to exotic, distant lands. Meet exciting, unusual people. And kill them." On the inside, Quinn rolled her eyes; why did liberals like him act as though people like her invented war and they alone wanted peace, love, and teddy bears? Quinn read his shirt again. Okay, maybe it was kind of funny. But it looked out of place on a guy who never smiled.

They had less than a minute before the bell rang, and the hallway had emptied out. He probably wouldn't acknowledge her; he never even said hi unless she said hi first. But he passed the classroom door. He was headed straight for her. His tan cheeks glowed bright pink, and his eyebrows scrunched together. Quinn felt her shoulders creep up as their eyes met. Was he going to call her out on something right now?

She saw Ilene slipping into the classroom and waved at her. Quinn tried to veer out of Seth's path; if he wanted to tangle, he'd have to wait until class, when Mr. Levine could referee. But he sidestepped in front of her, forcing her to stop. What the hell? They stared at each other for several seconds. Quinn noticed that the dark brown of Seth's eyes blended right into his pupils. He also had broad shoulders for a lean guy, but he was barely three inches taller than she was.

Seth started to say something but then kind of deflated. He pressed a limp, folded piece of notebook paper into her hand. Scowling at the floor, he mumbled something under his breath before charging into the classroom.

Quinn looked around in confusion to see if there had been witnesses. There hadn't. She walked into room 105. She sat down next to Ilene and said hi back to a few people. Taking a huge, slow breath, she slid the letter into her folder and pulled a pen out of her backpack.

Waiting for the slackers to trickle in, Mr. Levine strolled over to his desk and pried the lid off yesterday's McDonald's drink. He poured the light-brown liquid into the spider plant. Then he flipped off the lights and closed the door. He rubbed his hands together with that sinister glee that teachers saved for things like pop quizzes. Then he slapped an outline on the overhead projector, on which he'd chicken-scratched the title "South Africa." As the class groaned, Mr. Levine shrugged out of his sports jacket. He tossed it across his desk with one of the sleeves inside out.

As soon as he started talking about apartheid, Quinn flipped open her folder to read the note.

Dear Quinn,

Here's what I've wanted to say to you for a long time: I've liked you since the beginning of tenth grade. We haven't had any big conversations, but I feel like I know you.

I know that you're genuinely nice. Even though you

have a lot of friends, you make a point of saying hello to people like me (the shy, antisocial types!). You're really pretty, especially when you wear that green dress. You're also smart. I hear George Washington University figured that out, too. Congratulations on getting in.

I wondered if you'd like to go to a movie sometime. I know it sounds weird coming from someone you've barely talked to (and especially from someone who would tease you about being a Republican), but I hope you'll say yes.

Seth

Quinn closed her folder quickly and gazed at the lavender button-down shirt on the back of the guy in front of her. Not in a million years did she see this coming. She felt her cheeks burning as prickles of heat and sweat broke out on her back and neck. Thank God Mr. Levine had turned out the lights.

Seth didn't see her as a fraud. But he did see her. And he liked her anyway. It felt weird to be noticed without even realizing it.

At least having a boyfriend made a quick rejection easy to explain. Not that she had to explain herself. She sat up straighter in her seat and pretended to hang on Mr. Levine's every word.

"Apartheid means apartness in Afrikaans and Dutch," said Mr. Levine. He wrote down the word as he pulled his ugly gray stool near the overhead projector. It made a screech that made Quinn's toes curl. "Apartheid lumps people into strict racial groups and gives all the power to the whites."

The note felt like a setup; no matter what Quinn told Seth,

he'd think she just didn't date "guys like him." Even the truth would sound like an excuse to him. Then he'd probably feel all smug and vindicated as the martyr he already thought he was. Fine. She didn't care. Judging from the expression on his face, he already knew her answer. Quinn read the note again, noticing this time that its self-deprecating humor sort of let her off the hook. It was funny how a quiet person could open up in writing. Maybe it was possible to reject him without feeling as though she was kicking a stray puppy.

Ilene in the next seat over was smoothing on ChapStick and staring at her. Ilene had skipped second grade; she didn't miss a thing. Two rows beyond Ilene, Seth sagged in his seat with his eyebrows still clenched together.

CHAPTER 5
RADIOACTIVE

S itting ten feet away from Quinn in class, Seth wanted to barf. In the hallway, she'd looked at him like she was being jostled by a friendly but dirty dog. That her answer would be no was crystal clear; she'd blown him off before she'd even heard what he had to say.

He'd wobbled to his seat in the middle of the farthest row from the door. He figured that if he sat with his chin on his fists, he might be able to keep himself from puking or curling into the fetal position. Then he'd realized he could simply get up and leave before the bell rang.

The bell rang. He was trapped. Seth leaned his head sideways against the wall, stuck in hell. Why had he acted on this stupid idea, the Hail Mary pass of love letters? Seth stole a look in Quinn's direction. She was reading his note, her eyes wide. Christ. Seth flipped open his spiral notebook. The only thing he could do now was pretend to ignore her as she got ready to laugh in his face.

Seth scanned the room. Trish was doing a pencil rubbing of the Coach tag on her leather purse. In junior high, he and Trish had "gone together" briefly. That was back when they'd both been poor and had the single-mom thing in common. Their relationship had consisted of passing notes and making out under the stairwell. When she got a new dad and started moving up in the world, though, he'd dumped her preemptively; he could tell she was about to blow him off. They'd ignored each other ever since. Trish had walked right by him a few weeks ago in a deserted hallway and pretended not to see him.

Now he struggled to pay attention.

"South African blacks live in shacks on dirt roads with no heat or running water," said Mr. Levine. "Whites live in safe suburban houses with lawn services and cable TV."

Maybe taking notes would make him appear normal on the outside. Seth wrote, "apartheid = bad." Out of the corner of his eye, he saw Quinn yank a page out of her notebook. She crumpled it up and started writing again.

Seth kept his lunch down by concentrating on picking out the paper vertebrae from his notebook's distorted metal spiral. Why hadn't he stayed a coward? His work friends at the lumberyard—mostly older, muscled men—would have a good laugh over this one. If he told them. Which he wouldn't. He looked out the window. Today, the sun looked all innocent, but the wind mocked him with occasional gusts and whistles through a barely opened window. Someone had forgotten to wear deodorant. He checked; it wasn't him.

Mr. Levine threw his reading glasses—"cheaters," Seth's mom called them—onto the crowded desk and paced around the room. Ahead of Seth, a girl crossed her ankles, revealing cute calves. She wore long skirts and smelled like patchouli. One time, Seth had heard her rehearsing a piece for the speech team in the hallway. It was more like wailing—something about suicide and sparrows.

"Blacks lost their voting rights and the right to travel. Sound familiar?" Mr. Levine asked a huge football player in front of Drew. The guy fingered a gold square hoop in his earlobe.

"Jim Crow laws," he said.

"And when did the U.S. get out from under Jim Crow?" The football player sucked his teeth and scowled at Mr. Levine.

"Mm . . ." Mr. Levine nodded. "Yes, one could argue that we haven't. But how long has Jim Crow been illegal?"

"Twenty years? Twenty-five years?"

Again, Seth heard the sound of ripping notebook paper. When he looked at Quinn, she was staring right back at him. She crumpled the page, blushing again. She was uncomfortable? He was the one who was getting obliterated. Another blast of nausea hit him. A couple of weeks ago, *Exxon Valdez*, an oil tanker, had hit a reef in Alaska and created one of the worst environmental disasters in human history. This felt like that: a big fucking mess with no end in sight.

"Nelson Mandela and the African National Congress started a passive resistance campaign in the '60s. Parallels, Ilene?"

"Like our Freedom Riders and sit-ins," she said. That girl knew her stuff. Once Seth had heard Mr. Levine ask her about her plans after graduation. She'd said, "I'm going to Harvard," like you'd say "I'd like fries with that," and changed the subject.

"Good," said Mr. Levine. "But in South Africa, it didn't work. Citizen action doesn't always pay off."

No shit.

Seth had to be the first one out the door when the bell rang. Maybe by tomorrow he'd be able to piece together his shredded dignity, but he couldn't face Quinn again today. He sneaked another glimpse in her direction. She was reading whatever she'd written while crunching on her pen cap. He looked at the clock: ten minutes left. Mr. Levine sat back on his stool and clasped his fingers around one knee.

"President Botha uses guns and tear gas to stomp down blacks' strikes and boycotts," he said. Seth flipped a page to keep up with his fake note-taking. He wrote, "Botha (bwo-ta) = asshole." Mr. Levine stood up and stretched his arms over his head. "Back in the good old days, boys and girls, we called this fascism." He strode over and thwacked a manila folder against the lime-green poster tacked above Seth's head. Seth craned his neck to read it:

"Human beings the world over need freedom and security that they may be able to realize their full potential."
-AUNG SAN SUU KYI, BURMESE DEMOCRACY MOVEMENT

Mr. Levine scanned the classroom.

"How would you feel if you were a black South African right now? What do we know about people who have survived cruel leaders, foreign invaders, and civil wars? How does it feel to stand by as your family gets murdered and your children starve?"

The class only skipped one beat. "Really, really pissed off."

"And what are Americans doing about it?" Mr. Levine walked

to the blackboard on the class's left and peered up and down the metal tray. "My kingdom for a piece of chalk," he murmured. Drew reached behind some rolled-up maps on the tray and held up a white stub. As he handed it to Mr. Levine, he adjusted the blue-tinted black sunglasses that he'd perched on the top of his head. Seth hoped Drew's yearbook photo captured those gelled curls for all eternity. Mr. Levine nodded his thanks, then shouted at the class.

"C'mon! The whole world is pressuring South Africa to wake up and smell the democracy. Quinn, what's a sanction?" Seth's attention spun left. Quinn's snapped up from her notebook. She gave Mr. Levine a blank stare. "Would you like me to share your note with the rest of the class?" he asked, holding out his hand. Quinn's face mottled into an uneven shade of pink. Seth's head got ready to explode.

"No," Quinn whispered.

"Then put it away," said Mr. Levine. She slipped it into her folder.

Mr. Levine walked over to the front row desk in which Seth's friend Terrence was draped, sleeping, on his folded arms. Seth envied the peace of mind it would take to be able to sleep in a class. Terrence thought he fooled people by acting all L.L. Cool J with his baggy pants and swagger, but everyone knew he went to some kind of violin prodigy camp in the summer. Mr. Levine scanned the room, inviting the group in on his joke. Then he pounded on Terrence's desk. Terrence's head and each of his limbs flailed in a different direction.

"Terrence, you'll be interested to learn that President Reagan thought sanctions would mess up fair trade, so instead, he used a policy of 'constructive engagement' with the white government."

"That right?" Terrence asked, wiping drool on his sleeve.

"Yes. And that's not all, Terrence . . ." Mr. Levine's voice trailed off as he saw Quinn accidentally bumping Seth's folded note onto the floor. Seth watched in horror as Mr. Levine stepped in front of her and said, "Give it here, Quinn." He was mad now.

Christ. On. Crutches.

Quinn's eyes pleaded with Mr. Levine, but he kept his hand out until she gave him the note. The room hushed as he unfolded it and scanned it for a few seconds. The clock's second hand ticked like a hollow bomb. Mr. Levine stared at her hard. Folding it once, he gave it back.

"Put it away," he said. Seth let out a trapped breath.

"Sorry," Quinn whispered miserably. She crammed the note into her backpack. Mr. Levine glanced over at him with an unreadable expression. Seth felt each cell in his body screaming in abject humiliation.

"But American citizens like us," Mr. Levine said, looking pointedly at Quinn and Terrence, "thought Reagan was only sucking up to whites and ignoring blacks. So guess what we did?" Ilene raised her hand. Mr. Levine nodded at her.

"We boycotted U.S. banks so they'd stop lending money to South Africa," she said. "We made Congress pass sanctions, and we pressured American businesses to leave."

"Yes!" said Mr. Levine. "We've divested. We've raised hell. Citizen action has forced America to join countries like Sweden in demanding Mandela's release. It makes you proud, doesn't it,

Terrence?"

Terrence looked weary. "Yes, sir," he said.

"Can you think of other examples of citizens and corporations conducting American foreign policy?" The class was silent. "Me neither!" Mr. Levine crowed. "This is huge. The ground is shaking under our feet."

The bell rang. Mr. Levine walked over and flipped off the projector, leaving the classroom in near darkness.

Seth's heart pounded as he put his pen in his back pocket. He didn't care about any citizen's actions but his own. He darted past Mr. Levine, bumping his shin on the gray stool as he shot out of the room. Keeping his eyes on the pebbled floor of the hallway, he willed his numbed legs to move faster. He had to get the hell away from here.

He jumped at a light touch on his arm.

"Hi, Seth," Quinn said. She was forcing an anxious smile. It faded as she gave him a folded square of paper. Her hair swayed as she and her green dress turned around and rushed off in the opposite direction. Seth thumped against a rough hallway wall. He unfolded the note and read.

Dear Seth,

Thanks for being so honest and for the nice things you said in your note. I have a boyfriend. He goes to Southeast. We met in November.

You're smart, too. Mr. Levine acts like you're Jefferson himself and always tries to get you to share more pearls of wisdom. Are you two hatching some whiny liberal conspiracy? Don't you have some trees to hug?

I don't think being quiet is a bad thing. I've seen your face when Drew says something dumb. You look like you're entertaining yourself with a running commentary. I'm glad we don't sit next to each other. You'd probably make me laugh, and I'd get in trouble.

Your friend,
Quinn

Seth folded the note and slipped it into his pocket. He rested his head against the wall. Idiot! Of course, she had a boyfriend. He should have considered that. He shook out the paper again and smiled as he reread Quinn's reference to Drew. She did know he existed; she'd picked up on his sense of humor. Few people knew he was funny.

Shit. Seth stared at the pebbled marble floor, its aimless cracks patched with trickles of sanded grout. Getting to know her better hadn't actually been part of the note-giving plan. He hadn't expected to find substance beneath her warmth. Not that he'd thought she'd be shallow; he just hadn't thought. He slid down the wall to the floor and let the cold seep in.

CHAPTER 6
CONTAINMENT

After getting his ass kicked by a girl, Seth knelt by his battered locker and loaded his backpack full of books that he wouldn't have time to read. He zipped it, slung it over one shoulder, pulled up his jeans, and walked down the shadowy hallway. He ducked out of the school's west entrance, the one with the least foot traffic, the least resistance.

Seth kept his head down as he walked past the track field. Tidy little Lincoln frowned on litterbugs, but April sucked the potato chip bags and candy wrappers out of every crevice. It was kind of satisfying to watch them blow across the high school's crumbling asphalt parking lot in a loose mini tornado. It seemed like the crusty snow drifts had just melted, but now the weeds already jockeyed for position in the cracks in the cement. The trash and shredded wet leaves from last fall stuck together in heaps at the curb, like the soggy nests of huge, cynical birds.

As he walked the three blocks home, the sunshine broke through the pale clouds. It followed him, taunting him. At least spring was finally here. Winter in Nebraska meant that you coughed, blew your chapped nose, and had chronic hat head.

Virginia got cold sometimes in a wear-your-jacket-and-look-at-the-pretty-fog sort of way. But this was a hostile kind of freezing; it roared in from Canada, brought you to your scaly knees, and blew straight into your face. Seth and his mom used about a quart of lotion per day. You never knew when the dry air would shock you on a cat or the handle of the fridge. And you remembered Lincoln's steaming summers like a long-lost chapter of your childhood.

A year after Seth's parents had met at a war protest, a sniper killed his dad in Vietnam. Seth didn't remember him. Sometimes he hated him, though, for checking out instead of taking care of his wife and kid. Maybe then they could have afforded the rent in Washington, D.C. after the recession hit. When Seth's mom had accepted the landscaping job in Lincoln five years ago, she'd said she wanted to be within driving distance of her sister in her hometown of Des Moines. But she also wanted to be far enough away that she wasn't going backward—whatever that meant.

Seth stopped in front of his house. The sidewalk leading to it looked like a path of symmetrical icebergs frost-heaved into two-inch-high ramps and miniature gorges. This morning, night crawlers had stretched across the wet concrete like someone's guts. Now only fading wet spots, plus dozens of shriveled worm suicides hinted at last night's rain. Last week the brown grass had squished. Now it needed raking.

"Old-lady yard" is what his mom had called the two wasted little rectangles of hard-packed thatch on either side of the front walk. They'd barely stepped out of the U-Haul before she'd pointed out to him that the dense, prehistoric shrubs had scared off most of the grass. The peonies had collapsed by mid-June, a sad, pastel disaster. They grew where even a twelve-year-old landscaper's kid knew that sturdier plants belonged. She'd moved them to the back of the house, where they flopped in peace. With their cutesy balls of sugary pink, peonies still qualified as "old lady" in Seth's opinion, but he kept quiet; he'd seen his mom bury her face in them. The tea rose leaning against the rusting front spindles of the porch rail, on the other hand, hadn't stood a chance; Seth's mom hated tea roses. But she'd kept the window boxes, brushing off the faded cedar and filling them with ivy and white flowers.

The two of them had pissed off their neighbors first thing by chopping nine feet off the skeletal lilac hedge. But the Frankowskis liked Seth and his mom again now that the ten-inch stumps had morphed into four feet of privacy. The forsythia transplant to the backyard had been a total bust. It collapsed like a hundred-legged spider, a premature victim of the punishing Nebraska summer.

"I forgot about the fucking heat," his mom had said.

That sticky August, they had painted the kitchen that time forgot a bright sunflower yellow. They'd each guzzled sweating bottles of orange Crush. His mom had slopped coat after coat of paint onto the cracked seam between yellow wall and yellow ceiling. Her strawberry-blond hair frizzed through the back of her baseball cap and stuck to the sweat on her neck. The summer tan on her face skipped the crow's feet around her eyes, making them resemble tiny white sunbursts. Shouting the words to "Yellow Submarine" as the Beatles sang it on the boom box, she'd imitated John Lennon's sea captain cockney accent. Her scarred and callused hand swiped the wall with the clogged brush. At the demonic "Ah-ha!" at the end of the verse, she flicked her paintbrush at Seth. She covered him—cheek to ankle—in a yellow polka-dotted line while also knocking over her plastic tumbler of paint. It ricocheted off the side of the sink and flipped back onto the wall.

A quart of yellow paint streamed through a crack in the linoleum splash guard and disappeared. His mom made her eyes big. She blew out her breath in a loud, prolonged raspberry. Her small, muscled body doubled over, clinging to the counter as she laughed at his body-sized Nike swoosh of paint dots. Seth laughed, too, but he used the back of his mom's T-shirt to clean his face. It would take an hour to clean up this mess.

She eventually wound down. "Ah, fuck it." She raised a finger to signal a punch line. "That's the short form of the Serenity Prayer."

His mom hadn't had a drink in fifteen years. She joked that she'd majored in drugs before flunking out of college, but Seth couldn't picture it. The only traces he saw now of her partying days were the vertical smoker's lines around her mouth. The woman he knew practiced yoga and fed an addiction to Tootsie Rolls and bubble gum.

Two years after Seth and his mom moved in, she came home with a clematis vine in a shopping bag, its roots wrapped in a wet towel. They took turns standing on a borrowed ladder, hacking with an axe at the stringy, bloom-free wisteria vine crucified on the trellis under her bedroom window.

Seth couldn't remember a time when he didn't know way more

than he wanted to about gardening. Then again, any Virginian with a pulse knew what kind of grape-bunchy extravagance a wisteria was capable of. This wasn't it. They pulled out the roots and dumped compost into the hole. They planted the new vine. Seth went inside for candy and cold drinks.

When he came back, he found his mom sprawled at the base of the ladder. She wasn't hurt except for some scrapes on her elbows and forearm. But the look on her face was one of puzzled fear.

Then she started dropping things. They ignored the doctor's diagnosis at first, pretending that she didn't have MS. He researched primary progressive multiple sclerosis at the junior high media center only long enough to understand that it would ruin their lives.

Back then, she'd only used her ugly crutches with the beige cuffs on weekends. Now her body was falling apart so fast that Seth and she both existed in a state of constant, low-level anxiety. The disease surged occasionally, coming quickly and out of nowhere, like beatings. She was never not exhausted. Some nights, only her legs fell asleep.

On a visit to Des Moines a few years ago, Seth had overheard his aunt Gail ask his mom to name her worst fear. His mom's response had come fast and bitter: "That I'll wake up one day and realize I'm too helpless to kill myself." This knowledge had seeped into his pores.

On some level, he respected the idea of checking out on your own terms. But not when that idea involved the only member of his family. He asked her about it one time, theoretically speaking.

"My great aunt Breta always said, 'Aw, hell. It's a great life if you don't weaken.' And when she actually did weaken, she ended it," his mom said. "She found a lump and stopped eating."

"But that's terrible," Seth had said.

"No. She refused to be a burden to her family. I call that love."

He didn't bring it up again. His mom's calm death wish wafted away between crises, but the stink always seemed to come back.

On the porch now, he took the thin stack of mail from the rusting metal box. He unlocked the front door. His mom sat in her wheelchair right in front of the television, a concession to her fading eyesight. She used her elbow to push the off button, resting her limp hands on her still-muscled thighs.

"Hey, beautiful," she croaked. She probably hadn't spoken since that morning.

Seth leaned his backpack inside the door and walked over to her. He kissed her raised cheek, a relatively new ritual for them. The Bazooka bubble gum in her mouth cheered up the smell of her stale breath.

"What channel did you want?" he asked.

"I don't care," she said. "I have to pee so bad I was just trying to distract myself. Help me, will you?"

Seth tossed the mail onto the dining room table. The mushy smell of brown bananas on the kitchen counter reminded him of his earlier queasiness. He came back to the living room and grasped the wheelchair's ridged plastic handles, gliding it behind the couch and up to the edge of the shag carpet outside the bathroom door. The wheelchair outsized the doorframe by several inches. Seth planned to tear it out soon. In the meantime, he'd installed a rail along the wall so that his mom could get herself to the bathroom when she was desperate. She felt safer, though, when he helped her. That made two of them. As she stood and then inched along the rail beside him, she took up one of her favorite harangues. She pointed to his ratty Converse high-tops.

"We should grill outside tonight and put those ugly things out of their misery," she said.

Seth forced a smile. Sometimes he got sick of her teasing and sarcasm. But as long as she kept it up, he knew at least that her head was still in the game.

He gripped her under her armpits as she turned around and pushed down her sweatpants. He eased her onto the toilet. At this point, her tiny body was almost as familiar to him as his own. When he was younger, it mortified him to see her naked. Now he barely even thought about it.

"Hail to the queen," she said from her new raised old-person toilet seat. Seth squeezed out another feeble smile as his mom chatted over the sound of gushing pee. "Oprah had her fourth-grade teacher on today. She said something like 'I wouldn't be where I am today if Mrs. Duncan hadn't believed in me.'" Five years ago, his mom wouldn't have been caught dead watching daytime television. She poked him in the stomach. "Who crapped in your Cheerios?"

"Sorry," he said.

He avoided her eyes while passing her a wad of toilet paper but felt her watching his face. She backed off, thank God. He had to be alone. He helped her shuffle to the couch and sit down. In the kitchen, he made her a snack of sliced apples and iced tea. As he picked up her crossword dictionary from the dining room table, he saw an envelope from the ACT college admissions testing board. He folded it into his back pocket before his mom saw. His pulse pounded in his ears. He sorted through the other envelopes. It was all junk except for their monthly check, return addressed with the Fed's depressing Aid to Families with Dependent Children logo.

Needing the $338 a month felt so pathetic. His mom had quit landscaping after a series of near injuries on the job. The check on the table plus food stamps and a small stipend from Social Security would pay for a month's rent, cheap groceries, and expensive medications. Seth was finding that the recession was screwing up his tiny repertoire of meals; a few years ago, dinner had downshifted from chicken or hamburgers several times a week to Tuna Helper, beans and rice, and pasta. Going almost vegetarian saved about twenty dollars a month.

"I'll finish my homework and then make some dinner," Seth said.

His mom scrutinized him again over the back of the couch. "Take your time, honey," she said. "I'm not hungry."

He grabbed his backpack, noticing that the new strip of duct tape on the ripped side seam had already peeled back and acquired a grainy layer of grunge.

"*Cosby Show* tonight?" she asked.

"Sure." He went downstairs. Closing the door to his room in the basement's cool dampness, Seth pulled the ACT envelope out of his jeans and ripped it open. He'd scored a thirty. That put him in the top five percent in the country. Not that a high score changed anything; college was just not in the cards right now. Seth crushed the letter into a ball and hurled it into the trash. He flopped sideways onto his bed and unleashed a couple of pointless kicks at the cracks in the cinder block wall.

CHAPTER 7
THE IRON CURTAIN

Quinn took a left on Sheridan Boulevard as she walked home. On nearby Woodcrest Avenue, where Jason lived, gigantic trees draped their shade over mansions on deep, green one-acre lots. Quinn's mom sometimes referred to the Boulevard's "understated elegance." Quinn saw now for the first time the eroding sidewalks and scrubby grass by her own house. Her family's end of Sheridan looked like it was trying to morph back into prairie without anyone noticing. She wondered where Seth lived.

Her dad pulled up in the driveway in his Audi as she reached the front porch.

"Hiya, Ace. How was school?" he called up to her.

"Fine." She waited for him as he popped the trunk and pulled out his recent haul from Campbell's Nursery. He came up the wide front steps and set down a twenty-pound bag of potting soil and two huge flats of pansies on the low stucco wall of the porch.

Quinn knew his routine. He'd spend most of the evening pulling out the terra-cotta pots from the garage, brushing the crud out of them with his bare hands. Then he'd fill them with her mom's favorite flowers. When June came along and blow-torched the pansies, he'd replace them with hardier white geraniums. Barely a generation removed from the family farm, her dad distrusted people who didn't get dirt under their fingernails: real men dug up their own tree stumps.

Now he bent his tall, fit frame to scoop the afternoon edition of the newspaper off the doormat. He tucked it under his arm.

"Good," he said. He gave the back of Quinn's neck a friendly squeeze while jingling his keys. The smell of lemony cologne and cigarettes wafted off him like reassurance. He held open the door for her.

"How was work?" Quinn remembered to ask him.

"Not too bad," he said, his bright-blue eyes pleased. "Financial evaluations are kind of tedious but also necessary." Her dad's job as president of a local charitable foundation sounded fun on the surface, but giving away millions also involved a lot of paperwork.

"Oh," she said. "That stinks." Quinn had used the expression "that sucks" around her dad once. He'd stopped in his tracks.

"Do you know what the expression 'that sucks' means?" he'd asked her in a solemn voice.

"You know, 'Yuck, I hate it.'"

Her dad shook his head.

"I heard it all the time in the army. It's short for 'sucks a wad.' As in 'sucks a wad of ejaculate.' As in 'blowjob.' It's vulgar. Please don't say that again."

She hadn't. Ever. In front of anyone. Hearing the word *ejaculate* come out of her father's mouth had cured her. Gross.

Her dad made a beeline for his leather chair.

"Dad?" Quinn asked as he peeled open the *Lincoln Journal* and slouched down out of his workday.

"Mm . . . ," he replied after a minute, his eyes roving over the headlines.

Quinn perched on the hard-edged arm of the antique Stickley couch. As a kid, she'd woven polyester rainbow-colored yarn between its delicate square spindles.

"Why don't we belong to the country club?" she blurted. Yesterday, Jason had pointed out that they could spend time this summer at the pool if her parents joined.

Her dad folded the paper back down on his lap and peered at Quinn over the top of his glasses. His thick salt-and-pepper hair was growing out of a too-short haircut that accentuated the spreading patches of solid silver around his ears.

"Do you want to belong to the country club?" he asked.

"A lot of my friends belong." She shrugged. "Jason's family belongs."

"Can't Jason take guests?" The striped silk tie around her dad's neck was what he considered a walk on the wild side.

"Well, yeah, but I'd feel like a freeloader."

"Ah."

"Can't we afford to belong?" Quinn tensed now, wondering if she'd crossed the line into badgering. If she caught her dad at the wrong time, he'd stop playing devil's advocate with her and politely end the conversation. He rubbed his eyes with one freckled hand. She noted the blurred expression of a long day on his face. She'd have to tread lightly.

"We have the money," he said. "Friends asked your mother

and me to join years ago, and we declined. Do you know what a covenant is?" Quinn didn't. "It's when members of a private group make rules about who can and can't belong. Covenants allow gated neighborhoods to keep out the 'riffraff.' The Lincoln Country Club's covenant lets it exclude blacks and Jews and other minorities. Or at least it did twenty years ago. Your mother and I think that's crap."

"Oh." Quinn hadn't known that stuff was still legal twenty years ago. "Did you ever check to see if the covenant had been . . . you know . . . lifted?" It must have been if the Singhs belonged.

"No. In any case, I'd rather spend my money on something more interesting. I'm not a fan of groups that define who they are based on who they aren't. College Greek systems and fraternal organizations like the Masons do this. We all build walls to feel safe. But they often turn into traps that limit our experience. One might argue that the major religions do this. 'Ours is the only path to heaven' and all that foolishness."

A few years ago, after going with a friend to a confirmation class, Quinn had asked her dad whether he believed in Jesus.

"Sure," he'd said. "I think such a man existed. Jesus was as capable a prophet as any other. Like the rest of them, he told people to be nice and to help others. I do try to follow his example, however imperfectly. I pray first, though, at the church of democracy."

When she was little, while other families went to actual church, hers went to the consecrated, carpeted rooms of the Bennett Martin Public Library. But that was back when everything her dad said made perfect sense.

"What if the country club doesn't have a covenant now? What if it's not racist anymore? Or anti-Semitic?" Quinn asked.

Her dad sighed. "Being in a club is fun, I know. And God knows I need the golf practice." And the dance practice. Quinn had seen her parents at wedding receptions; their wine-buzzed head banging and twirling was painful to watch, like Ozzy Osbourne at a sock hop. "But we won't join the Lincoln Country Club on the principle that paying thousands of dollars a year to play in a rarefied social bubble is itself a kind of covenant, however informal," he said. "It's snobbish."

Quinn silently cataloged the zillion aspects of their lives that could already be called snobbish: her parents drove expensive cars and lived in an old, affluent part of town. But she let it go. Her dad, even while tired, could reason circles around her. If she kept going, she'd get emotional. Then he'd wave her away. Making a joke was the only way for her to back off with her dignity intact.

"So what you're saying is that you're a child of the Depression and that all you ever had to play with was a stick and a piece of string?"

When her dad laughed, his blue eyes crinkled at the corners. "That's right, smart-ass. Now let me read my paper."

Quinn returned his smile. She'd lost again. But she'd also regained a sense of calm. She could depend on certain things—like her philosophizing dad—to stay the same.

An hour later, Quinn sat on a chaise lounge on the deck, waiting for Jason to pick her up. Her parents let her go out on weeknights if she finished her homework first and came home by nine o'clock. The crowded hedges of lilacs and tall evergreen shrubs sheltered her from the breeze as she turned her face to the diluted light. Pulling up her knees to her chest gave her a warm buffer against the damp spring air. A scattering of pebbles landed at her feet. Jason poked his head around the side of the house.

"I was going to throw them at your window, but your mom said you were out here," he said, grinning at her. Only Jason could look sophisticated in a faded rugby shirt. He held out an eggplant.

"Gee, I'd been hoping for an eggplant," Quinn said.

"I figured," he said. "Ready?"

"*So* ready," Quinn said, pulling her cardigan off the back of the deck chair.

He took her to the Rotisserie, her favorite restaurant. Its white tablecloths, whimsical paintings of huge people, and homemade bread made her feel grown-up and at ease at the same time.

Jason put a small package in front of her. He'd wrapped a mixed tape in a scrap of an inside out grocery store bag.

"What's this for?" Quinn asked.

"Duh! It's our five-month anniversary!" He was making this up on the spot. They weren't the anniversary-celebrating types.

She giggled. "Right! Circled on my calendar," she said. She flipped over the tape and scanned the song titles written in Jason's scratchy print. The A-side was her Top 40 faves: The Police, The J. Geils Band, Michael Jackson, Prince, The Human League, Madonna, Eurythmics, and INXS. The B-side listed Jason's bands: New Order, Joy Division, The Smiths, R.E.M., The Fixx, Violent Femmes, The Cure, Led Zeppelin, and Grateful Dead.

"Two sides of the same coin?" she asked.

"Yin and yang," he said.

"That's profound. Peanut butter and jelly?"

"More like roast beef and marshmallow fluff," he teased. According to Jason, her taste in music was pathetically popular. Quinn didn't care; she thought his were pompous. Like his existence was so rough that he needed solace from his world-weary brothers in music? Please.

After dinner, they walked the brick-paved streets of the gentrifying Haymarket District. They bought ice cream cones. Jason swung her hand comfortably as they browsed in windows of antique shops and artists' studios. As they giggled at a particularly heinous brooch in a store's display case, a middle-school-aged black kid approached them with a cardboard tray of chocolate bars. He gave them a monotone speech about fundraising for his school. Then he asked them to buy a candy bar for a dollar. Midspiel, Jason turned back to the display window as though the kid were invisible.

Quinn scowled at Jason with a hand on her hip. He didn't notice. She dug in her pocket and paid the kid a dollar. He put a Hershey bar in her open palm and thanked her. As the boy walked away, Jason shook his head at her.

"Sweetheart, you got taken for a ride." His patronizing smile irritated her like a bulky sock seam.

"I'd rather be taken for a ride than ignore someone who might need my help." She licked her cone as she pretended to browse in the next store window.

Jason laughed. "Okay, Miss Social Conscience." He put an arm around her and hugged her from behind. "Let's go get a cup of coffee."

As they walked, her flats chafed against her bare heels. She sneaked a glance at his profile. Seeing him bite his ice cream hurt her teeth.

The next night, Quinn watched *Raising Arizona* on video with Jason and his parents. The four of them all squeezed together on the couch, eating a coffee-table picnic of samosas, Easy Cheese on celery, and Chips Ahoy. A few weeks ago, Quinn would have made herself at home. Tonight, the effort of pretending to want to be there felt exhausting. She left early.

When she got home, the house was dark and empty. Her parents had gone to a movie. Quinn headed straight upstairs and ran herself a bath, her favorite way to let off steam. She shuddered as she eased herself into the hot water and bubbles. She fantasized about Seth and the warm, wet places she wanted him to go. The hand that had taken her note yesterday had had tiny scrapes and scratches on it. The light tan on Seth's forearms ended right before the rolled-up cuffs of his shirt sleeves. Quinn shuddered again as her fingers found her sweet spots, coming so fast and hard that a mini tidal wave of bubbles and water splashed onto the tile floor.

It never felt this good with Jason.

CHAPTER 8
DÉTENTE

The next morning, Quinn sat on the living room floor with her elbows on the coffee table, studying the newspaper's headlines for class. Both of her parents had early meetings.

"What's going on?" her dad asked, gesturing at the paper as he straightened his coat collar. He read the morning paper at work.

"Three hundred thousand pro-choice activists marched on Washington," Quinn said.

"What did she say?" her mom asked as she rushed down the stairs. Quinn hated it when she did this, charging into conversations that were half-over. Her mom ran an entire public relations firm plus most of their household. She was a doer. It wasn't clear if Quinn was a natural daddy's girl or if she'd become "his" kid by default. Sarah had always needed and gotten more of their mom's time: her failing grades and daily dramas called for a doer. Her mom pivoted on one pump-clad foot three times on the wood floor of the center hallway as she searched for her briefcase.

"She said that a swarm of three hundred thousand lesbians and angry women descended on D.C.," her dad said. He pointed to Quinn's mom's briefcase wedged between two spindles of the banister. He waited for his wiseass remark to sink in.

"Watch it," her mom told him. She swatted his butt.

"Overgrown flower children?" he suggested.

Quinn frowned.

"I think you mean 'Americans that are carrying the water for lazy pro-choice individuals,' such as yourself," her mom told him.

"All right," her dad said mildly. He held the door for her. They waved goodbye and left.

Quinn listened to the sudden, carpeted silence for a second before standing up. She threw the newspaper on her dad's chair, where it scattered into a loose heap. Why did he have to make the march on Washington sound silly simply because the protesters were women? The abortion issue wasn't really Quinn's thing either. But she was paying enough attention to notice that pro-lifers were trying to roll back *Roe v. Wade*. Besides, Quinn had enough to worry about without her dad hopping up and down on her last nerve.

Trish pounded a heart-stopping greeting on Quinn's stall that afternoon in the echoing girls' bathroom.

"Hey! Tonight let's go to *Heathers* and Imperial Palace. I'm craving some—"

"Crab Rangoon, I know," Quinn interrupted, adjusting her slip. She opened the door. "Fine, but we're getting two orders this time." Quinn was on intimate terms with her best friend's premenstrual syndrome: stay away from Trish's plate full of greasy MSG, and no one gets hurt.

"Rude!" Trish's shout competed with a flushing toilet echoing against ceramic tile. She disappeared into the next stall.

Fast, high-pitched conversations like these drove Quinn's dad insane. More than once, he'd pointed the television's remote control at Quinn and Trish as they talked over each other, pretending to turn down their volume.

They met at the sinks. Trish wore her "Cure AIDS" button today on the lapel of her shoulder-padded pink blazer. Her favorite uncle, Matt, had AIDS. Last summer he'd taught them both how to make corn tortillas from scratch. He owned a real tortilla press.

"How's Matt?" Quinn asked. The update always hurt to hear.

"Skinny. Tired. He's getting sores on his face, says he feels like the poster child for domestic abuse prevention."

Quinn squeezed Trish's wrist. Scientists had just discovered that the AIDS virus could become resistant to AZT. In other words, if Matt stopped responding to the drug, he'd die.

No time today for the hand dryers. They wiped their wet palms on their clothes and jostled each other out of the bathroom. The hallway clock gave them twenty seconds before class started.

"Remind me who's in *Heathers*?" Quinn asked. They walked fast.

"Winona Ryder," Trish said. She pushed up the sleeves of her blazer to reveal a jangle of thin silver bracelets.

Quinn trailed in her wake until they cleared the hallway doors. Then they broke into the daily race: them against the bell, them against each other. She pulled even with Trish as they careened down the worn marble staircase. They cleared the bottom step at the same time.

"Is Winona the whiny one from *Beetlejuice*?" Quinn asked as they zigzagged across the hall. "The girl who thinks she's so adorable she doesn't have to act?"

"You'll love it, genius girl. And you're going to spare me your intellectual snob bullshit," Trish said, pushing Quinn ahead of her into room 105. They skidded into their seats as the bell rang.

Ilene sat poised to take notes on lined paper in her spotless Trapper Keeper with her right hand while nibbling a cuticle on the left. Thirty seconds later, Seth slouched into the room, carefully ignoring Quinn's half of it. She fought the blood rushing to her face. She sat up straighter, knocking a book onto the floor.

"What's going on with you?" Ilene half whispered out of the side of her mouth. She picked up the book and handed it to Quinn with a square of Hershey bar on top of it. Ilene kept her eyes on Mr. Levine, who was brushing little chunks of potting soil off a stack of papers. "You're acting weird."

Quinn ate the chocolate. She tried to think of a good excuse. But she surprised herself by unloading in a whisper. "I got a love note yesterday from Seth Burton," she said.

Ilene scrutinized Quinn's face. She finally nodded, as though a declaration from Seth Burton fell within her range of normal.

"And?"

"And I have a boyfriend, remember?"

Ilene nodded. She and her boyfriend were one of those sweet, comfortable couples that would make you want to puke your guts out if you didn't know they were doomed. Her parents didn't even know she'd been dating a *goy* for a year, let alone that he was a religious one. "Caleb's mom barely speaks to me," Ilene had told Quinn once. "She thinks I personally participated in Jesus's crucifixion."

Today, in her standard khaki pants, white shirt, and simple silver necklace, she looked particularly like the least dangerous person in the world.

"Hmmm . . . Too bad," said Ilene, glancing in Seth's direction. "He's wicked smart."

Mr. Levine interrupted their whispered conversation. "Are you two ready to join us?" He was looking straight at Quinn but smiling.

Quinn's stomach skittered. Ilene started twirling her bangs into dense ringlets, a nervous habit. More than once she'd presented a debate-tournament rebuttal with mini dreadlocks sprouting from her forehead.

"What do we do with the fact that many of South Africa's black resistance groups are communists?" asked Mr. Levine. "And terrorists? Seth?"

Now Quinn's stomach started to churn.

"They don't have much of a choice since the U.S. won't help them," Seth said. "If we really cared about spreading democracy, we'd help the black majority run the country."

Did he feel as wobbly as she did on the inside, or was he one of those aggravating guys who somehow kept their classes and their emotions separate?

"If blacks ran the United States, we'd be talking to the African National Congress?" asked Mr. Levine.

"Yup," said Seth.

Being personally humiliated apparently didn't keep him from reading the newspaper and cranking out informed opinions.

Quinn sneaked a glance at him. He liked the band U2, judging from the doodling on his frayed binder. She knew plenty of people who thought U2 was cool: people who liked boring guy music. Dark circles framed Seth's eyes today. She saw anxiety lines on his forehead, too, when he brushed away his overgrown hair.

"Who agrees?" asked Mr. Levine.

Quinn raised her hand. What the hell. She saw Seth notice.

"Why do you keep asking us what would happen if special interest groups ran the country?" Drew asked.

"How do you define 'special interest group'?" a girl asked Drew. Her avalanche of white beaded braids sighed a chorus of clicks every time she turned her head.

"You know, blacks, Palestinians, women. All those groups Mr. Levine throws at us," Drew said.

"President Bush?" the girl asked.

"What about him?" Drew said.

The girl sighed. "What's his special interest group?"

"He's not in one. That's what I'm saying," Drew explained.

Seth snorted.

"Seth?" said Mr. Levine.

Seth turned to glare at Drew and caught Quinn looking at him. She carefully considered the Cambodian guy's head in front of her. She wondered if he was aware that he had paid hard-earned cash for a bowl cut.

"Everyone belongs to a special interest group," Ilene said. "No one's neutral, especially not politicians."

Quinn understood suddenly that this was true. Her dad's arguments began and ended with the assumption that he was neutral and everyone else had an agenda. Until this second, it hadn't occurred to her how arrogant it was to think of yourself as neutral.

"I don't buy it," Drew muttered. He sounded, though, like he just didn't want to.

The breeze through a half-open window brought in the damp smell of last night's rain. It was one of those dissatisfied early spring days that tried on weather like girls tried on outfits. Dense gray clouds crouched for a minute or two over the school's parking lot. Then they wandered off in search of a better space.

"Seth," said Mr. Levine, "do you agree that the United States is helping end apartheid even if we're only talking to whites?"

"I guess," Seth said. "But then again, it's kind of a joke for Americans to make demands on Botha's government. We act like we're a model of tolerance here, but we're not." Seth glared at Quinn with his jaw clenched. She heard the personal accusation as if he'd said her name out loud. She turned to face him. He could take his manipulative argument and shove it.

"America isn't perfect," she said to Seth, "but what would happen if we didn't talk to South Africa? I bet six million Jews would have welcomed more intervention from our imperfect democracy." She glared at him. "And why is it okay to whine about tolerance and sneer at the rest of us? You think it's lame for us to criticize South Africa. But I think it's lame for you to criticize Reagan's policies. The only reason we're having this discussion is because the Cold War is ending. Democrats like you sit around and talk about peace while Republicans actually go out and get it."

She slumped back in her seat, flipping angrily through her notebook and pretending to look for an empty page. Who the hell did he think he was giving her notes that made her feel like he knew her, like her regular life wasn't good enough? Her fingers shook to the same beat as her heart.

Seth was looking right at her. Practically every muscle in his arms and chest stood out when he sat up straight like that. He offered her a tiny smile with one eyebrow raised, a mock salute. Was he actually being a good sport? Surprised, she grinned back. The last thing she'd expected from Seth Burton was a glimmer of solidarity. When he didn't wear that wary, haunted expression, he was even sort of cute.

CHAPTER 9
CONVENTIONAL WARFARE

Through the sliding glass door in the breakfast nook of their kitchen that afternoon, Quinn saw her parents lounging on padded deck chairs, drinking beer from green bottles. Her family spent every possible minute outside during the few months that didn't qualify as scorching summer or face-numbing winter. Quinn dumped her backpack on the linoleum. She took a Coke and a pizza slice out of the refrigerator.

On the deck, she waved a silent hello and flopped into a damp chair. Kicking off her shoes, she added her own white feet to the four already crowding the padded footstool. Their legs formed the spokes of a half wheel of tired people on a Friday afternoon.

The sun broke through the clouds again, warming Quinn's face. Spring had sprung; purple hyacinths huddled together in their sheltered clumps. Quinn had helped her dad plant the bulbs. Daffodil greens stretched their inevitable fingers toward the sky. The forsythia near the gate got ready again to take over the universe. Elvis, the cat, stretched out on a sun patch. Her dad's latest paperback sat underneath his chair, waiting for him to finish his cigarette. Quinn sighed.

"Long day?" her mom asked. She had tossed her tortoiseshell up-do clip next to the ashtray. She scooped her blond hair up and over the back of the chair. Her toes sported fresh pink polish. Quinn swallowed her bite of pizza. Next door, someone screeched open a grouchy-sounding window.

"The longest," Quinn said. She recognized her parents' expectant silence as a tactic, but she took the bait anyway. She'd spent these past few days feeling almost entirely composed of self-righteousness and pent-up adrenaline; she had to spend it somewhere.

"Dad, did you know that Reagan supported apartheid?" she asked.

Her father took a long swig of beer. "How so, Ace?" he asked, keeping his face neutral. He wore his horrible plaid shorts and an old sweatshirt. Its faded red color didn't quite match the red in the plaid. In a way, he was still that verge-of-hunger farm kid; he wore his clothes to shreds.

"Reagan only talked to the white government. And at the UN, he voted against sanctions," Quinn said.

Her dad gave her his crinkled blue-eyed smile. "Is this the public education we support with our hard-earned tax dollars?" he asked.

Quinn's mom cleared her throat and blew a strand of hair out of her wide brown eyes. This was code for "I'm not in the mood for another political go-around after a long work week."

"What your dad means is that Reagan's policies were more layered than that," she said.

"Right," her dad said, squeezing her mom's knee and ignoring her nonverbals. "Reagan thought friendly communication was the best way to get the Afrikaners to change. He actually had a better relationship with South Africa than any other American president."

If Quinn played by her dad's rules, she knew she'd be able to show him that Reagan was a racist. He frowned on racists.

"But, Dad, Reagan could have done a lot more if he'd talked to both sides," she said.

Her dad slid down farther in the cushioned deck chair, nudging one of Quinn's feet off the foot stool by pretend accident. Quinn's mom let out a groan, swigged her beer, and leaned her head back again on her chair cushion. She closed her eyes.

"Reagan should have talked to blacks—in public—as much as he spoke to the whites," Quinn said. "I mean, you said the Lincoln Country Club's covenant was wrong. So why do you side with the whites in South Africa?"

Her dad's smile faded. "Reagan didn't deal with the black resistance for moral reasons," he said. "Most of them turned communist, Quinn. They're still getting money and guns from the Soviet Union."

Mr. Levine had said something about communists helping the black resistance. But like Seth had pointed out, why not let them? How bad could communists be if they were helping get rid of apartheid? For once, it was easy to tell who the good guys were. Quinn thought about how to phrase this to her dad. She watched a speckled woodpecker making his way around a nearby telephone pole, drilling into the soft spots.

"The Cold War isn't over, Quinn," her dad said. "We still need a democratic ally in Africa."

"But South Africa isn't a democracy!" Quinn said.

Her mom opened one eye and squinted it at Quinn. She rolled up the cuffs of her faded jeans, exposing toned, olive calves. "Can Jason join us for dinner?" she asked. "I'm making that rib recipe he likes."

Quinn had no idea what Jason was up to tonight. She hadn't returned his last call. "No, he has other plans."

"Sarah called, by the way," her mom said. "She got a callback for an off-Broadway dance thing."

Quinn wanted to hear more, but not now. Leave it to Sarah to derail a conversation that she wasn't even in.

"That's great. I knew she'd get it," her dad said. He turned back to Quinn. "You're right," he acknowledged carefully. "I meant 'democratic' as in 'not communist.' But you have to appreciate, Quinn, that this is a gray area. Reagan did his best in a terrible mess. And by encouraging the Afrikaners to start a real dialogue with the United States, he helped them see that reasonable people can disagree and still be friends. He was against sanctions because he knew that making South Africa's economy shaky would make it even more unstable politically." He almost sounded like Mr. Levine. Quinn was losing her thread. Her dad stubbed out his cigarette. "When the apartheid regime falls—and I think you're right, it has to at some point—we'll thank Reagan for being one of the reasons why."

One tiny helping of vindication tasted so right that Quinn had to go back for more. "I think we'll thank him for making us seem like racist jerks," she said. "If it weren't for Congress going over Reagan's head and sanctioning South Africa, we'd look like we didn't learn anything from the civil rights movement."

She remembered Seth's little smile at her at the end of today's class. What would he think of this conversation? Her dad made a funny face at her. He was spinning a rebuttal in his head. Quinn slapped at a biting insect on her upper arm. She felt a twinge of regret as a ladybug clicked to the ground. She tapped her fingers on the arm of her chair.

"Besides," she said, "It's stupid not to deal with black resistance groups just because some of them are communists. They see themselves as oppressed workers. So what? Apartheid is real. Communism's only . . . like . . . a theory."

Her mom's eyes popped open. Her dad's smile faded as his eyes narrowed.

"Only a theory?" he asked, straightening up in his chair. He looked like he was about to take a bite out of her. "Hitler gassed twelve million people during World War II. Do you know how many Stalin killed in the Soviet Union alone?" Quinn shook her head. "Twenty million! At least! Do you have any idea how many people have been tortured and murdered in the last seventy years as a result of Soviet communism?"

She didn't. For the sake of this argument, she'd downplayed in her head the horror stories she'd heard her whole life. Her dad was right. But she was right about the hypocrisy of Reagan only talking to whites. She knew it. Pushing her dad this far, though, made her feel slightly ill, like she was glimpsing a busy street from a high ledge. But if she calmed herself down now, she knew she could get him to see what she meant. A heap of thick gray clouds piled on the horizon, getting ready to unload.

"How about another beer, Tom?" her mom asked as she half rose from her chair.

"I'll get it," he said. He scowled. Exhaling slowly, he went inside.

"No one disagrees with you, Quinn, that apartheid is terrible," her mom said quietly as she leaned back in her chair. "But you can't pretend that the resistance is a bunch of heroes. They're not. They're terrorists. Nelson Mandela—the glorious martyr to the cause—is a terrorist." A small zap of distant lightning tried to reinforce her mom's words, but Quinn had climbed onto sturdier moral ground now. She knew a thing or two about the civil rights movement; it took more than passive resistance.

"Wouldn't you use violence, too, if nothing else worked? And wouldn't you let the Soviets help you if America wouldn't?" she asked. She wondered why her parents couldn't take the truth at face value. Wasn't the simple, obvious answer ever the right one?

"You can't justify terrorism, Quinn. Violence is not the answer," her mom said. Quinn's dad returned with two beers. He nudged the sliding door shut with his big toe. Quinn gripped the arms of her deck chair.

"But what about what the Afrikaners do to blacks? How . . ." She stopped herself. Would winning this argument feel any better than losing it? She didn't need to win, not really; she only wanted her dad—for once—to bend his thinking a little. She wanted to stay on the same team. Sitting down again, her father put his fingertips together and closed his eyes as if to compose himself.

"I understand what you're saying, Quinn. I share your outrage at the awful things blacks suffer in South Africa. It's unthinkable." Quinn relaxed slightly. Their views weren't so different. "But when South Africa emerges from this terrible mess," he continued, "Americans will benefit from Reagan's policies, especially economically."

Quinn pictured the yellowing poster on Mr. Levine's wall:

> ## "You can depend upon the Americans to do the right thing. But only after they have exhausted every other possibility."
> ### -WINSTON CHURCHILL

New frustration erupted in her chest.

"You said Reagan was 'engaging' the whites for moral reasons. But now you admit that it's about money!" she shouted.

Her father leaned forward and stabbed a finger at her. "Listen!" he shouted back. He regained control of his voice. "I'm glad you're paying attention at school. I'm glad you have teachers who make you think. But you can't go around acting like you're the first person to discover injustice. Try on some liberal ideas if you like, but remember, too, that the Left hasn't cornered the market on moral outrage!" Her mom sat very still. Quinn's chair grated hard as she leaped to her feet. Her dad stood up, too, with a frustrated scowl, and blocked Quinn's way. His tight, white lips made her dread what came next. "Politics are messy, Quinn," he said, disgust in his voice. "Your emotional grab for black-and-white answers makes you sound like a child."

"Tom," Quinn's mom said in a low, warning voice. "Quinn,"

she continued, "what your dad means is that looking at the economic side of things doesn't make people like us bigots or cynics. It means we recognize how the world works."

Quinn ignored her and glared at her dad, hot faced and shaken. She clunked down her pop can and yanked open the sliding glass door. Once inside, she slammed it behind her as hard as she could. A slight popping sound made her look down. As she watched, a small crack formed at the base of the frame. On the other side, her mom's eyes darted from the crack to Quinn's face. Her expression said that the line had been crossed. Quinn bolted upstairs to her room.

CHAPTER 10
ALLIES

"**I** was robbed!" Seth's cousin Lee shouted that night before trying to steal back the basketball.

Seth faked to Lee's left and ran to his right. He breezed a long shot into the basket. "Someday, son, you'll be a ballplayer like me," he said, reaching up to squeeze the back of Lee's neck. Two years older and several inches taller than Seth, Lee usually crushed him while barely breaking a sweat. Lee let Seth savor his victory for two seconds before smacking the ball away from him and starting game three.

Lee's mother, Gail, was Seth's mom's sister, the one who knew her worst fear. Gail could only make the three-hour drive about once a month; her house, husband, cashier job, and younger kids kept her busy in Des Moines. Seth's mom squawked—but not very convincingly—when Gail came and spent half the weekend scrubbing their floors and freezing meals. These visits saved Seth, though; he barely kept up with the daily chores and grocery shopping, let alone his paying job and his homework. And he loved hearing the two sisters bicker and laugh over the best way to fold fitted sheets, or whatever. Lee came along with Gail every two or three months when he got time off from Sears.

Lee's boom box sat on the low cinder block wall that divided the backyard from the alley and the near-empty, slumping excuse of a one-car garage. It pulsed music by some obscure California punk rock band that Lee had just discovered. Below the boom box, hidden by some weeds, sat a carton of four cold beers and two empty bottles.

"What's the name of this group?" Seth asked.

"Sweet Children," Lee said. "Actually, no. They changed it. Now they're Green Day. They just released this album, but only on vinyl."

"Wait. Seriously?"

"I know! Who does vinyl anymore? A friend in California sent me this tape."

"No. I mean, this is Green Day?"

"Yeah. Why?"

"My friend Terrence invited me to his house tomorrow to hear this totally obscure band called Green Day. His brother is friends with the drummer or something. They're on their first tour, and his brother got them to stay a night in Lincoln."

Lee stared at him. "Are you fucking kidding me?" he asked. Seth shook his head. "What did you tell Terrence?"

"I said I didn't think I could make it. But I guess I just changed my mind?"

Lee grinned. "You got that right." He passed the ball to Seth. "You look like shit, by the way. Don't you ever sleep?"

"I sleep."

"Under a rock? On a rock? You need a haircut, too. Like I said, you look like shit."

"Thanks." Seth threw the ball at Lee's chest and lunged to block him.

"For real, what's up?" Lee asked a few shots later, avoiding Seth's eyes.

Seth pretended to think.

"Well, geez, you can only body surf mosh pits so often before it catches up with you." He sighed. "That and my mom started wetting her pants." Lee waited for him to go on. "I have to start making her wear diapers. But even the idea embarrasses the hell out of her."

"That sucks," Lee said. He did a quiet lay-up. "What else?" he pressed, bouncing the ball to Seth. "What's her name?"

Damn. The flip side of being understood by someone was that you didn't get away with squat. Seth dribbled the ball three times, four.

"Quinn."

Lee studied his face. "She cute?"

"Yup."

"She know you exist?"

"In a dishearteningly asexual kind of way. But yes. I gave her a note."

Lee stopped smiling. "What did it say?" He held the ball against his hip with his forearm.

"That I like her and want to take her out." Seth studied the rusted rim of the hoop.

"And?"

"And she was nice about it. She has a boyfriend. I'm screwed."

"You wish you were." Lee grinned, hurling the ball at him.

"Correct," Seth said. At this rate, he'd never get laid. He faked a shot before launching it over Lee's head. Swish.

At least on a basketball court Seth knew who he was—he understood what he was up against. The rest of the time, he didn't know what the hell he was doing. He got blindsided by crap that didn't even occur to him to anticipate. Why hadn't he just dropped the stupid class when Quinn had turned up on the first day? It wasn't like he needed the credits. Or would use them.

After dinner, Seth, his mom, Lee, and Aunt Gail flipped channels on the television, waiting for *Dallas* to come on at eight o'clock. Seth had possession of the clicker. He paused on the news. The anchorman reported that Iraqi president Saddam Hussein had killed fifty to one hundred thousand Kurds with chemical weapons and mass executions.

"Jesus," Seth's mom said. "Poor souls." She always talked back to the television.

The news anchor in his dark suit changed topics and camera angles. "In the wake of the recent Soviet withdrawal from Afghanistan," he announced, "Afghan communists are now taking over the city of Jalalabad." They watched the footage of dusty, violent chaos.

"What happens to all those angry mujahideen now?" Seth's mom asked. "They've got nothing but Allah, rubble, and American AK-47s."

Gail shook her head. Lee drummed a beat on his lap with a rolled-up magazine.

"Mr. Levine has a theory," Seth said.

"Yeah?" said his mom. "Let's hear it."

"He thinks that when people live in poverty and violence, they get really, really pissed off."

"Wow, dude, that's deep," Lee snorted.

"I'm not done," said Seth. "He says we should help out with food and education and medicine wherever it's needed—communist or not. That supporting human rights in unstable countries primes them for democracy. That creating stability builds markets for American capitalism. Like it's a win-win, see?"

"He said that?" Seth's mom asked.

"Yep."

"In class?"

"Well, not exactly in class. But to me."

She smiled. "I knew I liked that guy."

Seth and Lee shot hoops again later in the twilight. After they'd parked the basketball in the grass next to the fence, they stood at the kitchen sink and pounded down tall glasses of tap water. The window looked out over the "verandah." The former owners had forgotten to press seams into the concrete patio when they poured it; by now, decades of freezing and thawing had broken it into shifting pieces. It was so lame that Seth and his mom had decided to glorify its lameness. They'd furnished it with a peeling metal folding chair, an ugly purple Adirondack rescued from a garage sale, and an overturned ten-gallon bucket covered in checked picnic-table vinyl. Home sweet home. From the kitchen window, you got an eyeful of crabgrass growing out of the cracked cement.

This morning's creepy green storm haze had eased into just

another day. As the sun set now, it cast a peachy glow, making the yard appear slightly less like the Joads' from *The Grapes of Wrath.*

"That's crazy, what you did," Lee said. "You should never put that shit in writing."

Seth farted long and loud in Lee's direction. "I figured that out on my own, O Wise One."

"But at least now you know."

"Right. Now I know."

The next morning, Seth stacked heavy sheets of plywood on metal shelves in the cavernous storage area of the lumberyard. Sawdust clung to his hair and sweaty bare arms above his leather gloves. His coworkers made fun of him for switching to short sleeves so early in the season—and for not wearing a cap—but he'd rather itch than die of heatstroke.

Seth and four other guys took their coffee break together every Saturday. Actually, no one drank coffee. Seth drank Dr. Pepper while the older men—in their thirties and forties—broke out their smokes. They sat in the dusty break room, on an old door propped on sawhorses. One guy settled back in a folding chair. Pushing up his flannel sleeves, he started flapping his hands and imitating the lispy voice of a flamboyantly gay guy who'd just stopped in for precut picket fencing. Seth smiled in spite of himself at his co-worker's perfect mimicry.

"Did you hear what AIDS stands for?" another guy broke in. They all shook their heads as he took a deep drag on his cigarette. "'Adios, Infected Dick Sucker!'" Loud laughter erupted. Seth jumped to his feet, knocking over his can of pop.

"Shut the hell up," he said. "That's not funny." People rarely surprised Seth—one of the benefits of keeping his expectations low. But he respected these guys. He'd thought they were too cool for this kind of bullshit.

"Aw, lighten up, Seth," one of them teased. "He's only joking."

They all watched him—amused—like he was a toddler throwing a tantrum. Seth strode out of the break room, leaving the puddle of Dr. Pepper for them to clean up. As he searched for his supervisor to get his next assignment, he found Mr. Levine standing in the paint section.

"What's up, Mr. Levine?"

"Seth! I'd hoped I'd run into you. What do you know about paintbrushes?"

"What are you painting?

"Everything, actually. I bought a new house yesterday."

Seth smiled. "You've come to the right place then. I can hook you up." He pointed out the basic rollers hanging on the rough pegboard and a high-quality brush for trim work. "Don't skimp on the paintbrush. It's gonna be your best friend." Mr. Levine nodded, totally confused. He grabbed everything Seth recommended.

"By the way," Mr. Levine said, "I asked the school counselor about college loan applications. She's going to put together a stack for you."

Seth studied the edging tools. "Thanks."

"It's like taking the ACT, Seth," Mr. Levine said seriously. "Do it now so that you have it in your back pocket. Even if it takes you five years to make it happen, it's still waiting for you."

Seth got it. But this stuff took time and energy. Right now, he had neither. Sometimes he wished Mr. Levine believed in him less. "It's not like going to college guarantees me a perfect life or something." He gestured at the shop and its sawdusty floor. "I like working here. Besides, I'd rather have callused hands and work for minimum wage for fifty years than be a partner in the firm of Trust Fund, Silver Spoon, and Sellout."

Mr. Levine broke out in a broad grin. "I see. Are you finished?"

"I guess."

"I think you're throwing the baby out with the bath water."

"How so?"

"Not to put too fine a point on it, Seth, but acting against your own self-interests to piss off the establishment or whatever is stupid. If my hippie days taught me anything, it's that the establishment doesn't give a damn about your silly little life. You have to make it as good as you can, because no one else is even paying attention."

"You're saying that the men who work here don't lead good lives?"

"Not at all. I'm saying . . . um . . . Can you keep a secret?"

"Sure."

"I'm getting married. We're having a baby."

"No kidding? That's excellent!"

"Thanks. Yes, we're really excited. Sort of terrified, too, but mostly excited. I'm sharing this with you, though, because I have this sudden, fresh appreciation for my education and earning power. I feel lucky to be semi-equipped for this . . . unexpected blessing. Seth, I get it that you've decided who you're not. But who have you decided to be?"

Seth briefly mulled over his conversation with Mr. Levine as he spent the rest of the day learning how to operate the forklift. Mostly, though, he thought about the night ahead; his plan was to forget this whole week by listening to good music and getting wasted.

CHAPTER 11
DISARMAMENT

The band was playing in Terrence's garage. He lived east of town off Old Cheney Road. A muscled guy wearing acid-washed jeans and a mullet stood at the door and waved them in. There were no signs of Terrence's parents. Quinn didn't recognize anyone until they headed to the crowded basement to locate the keg. The warm room already smelled like pot and beer. Terrence shouted introductions between Trish, Quinn, and a tall guy named Lee. He also confiscated Quinn's car keys.

"My brother's orders!" he yelled over the noise of fifty or sixty bodies crammed into a room. Then he filled their "Go Big Red" plastic tumblers with beer.

"Didn't catch your name!" Lee shouted into Quinn's ear across the tub of melting ice. Terrence drifted off to collect more car keys.

"Quinn," she shouted back. "And you're Lee?" She knew his name was Lee. She simply couldn't think of anything else to say. He looked at her closely. Stared, actually.

"Quinn, you said?" he asked.

She nodded politely. Then she mouthed, "Nice to meet you,"

before moving away. Trish had already disappeared, a recurring party issue between the two of them.

Trish couldn't have gone back upstairs without her noticing, though. Quinn squeezed through loud conversations and sloshing beer to stand on the bottom stair step. From here she had a better view of the crowd. No Trish, though. Lee still stood by the keg, checking her out.

Quinn spied a sliding glass door that led out to a patio or yard. The good thing about faking a nicotine habit, she'd discovered, was that it gave you an excuse to get away from loud parties and boring small talk. She made her way across the room and pulled open the door just wide enough to squeeze through.

The pitch-dark made her blind. She stepped out of the rectangle of light streaming from inside and put her hands in the pockets of her jean jacket. As her eyes got used to the dark, she saw that the house overlooked a small lake. A deep blue bowl of sky seemed to hold the stars barely beyond her grasp, like a piece of canvas holding back helium balloons. She let herself exhale.

Someone cleared his throat from three feet away. Seth stood up, a fellow party refugee. He brushed grass off the back of his jeans with one hand. In the other he held an empty beer cup. He smiled apologetically and flashed her a half-hearted peace sign before moving past her to go back inside.

Quinn didn't think. She grabbed the front of his shirt and kissed him hard. A few seconds later, she pulled back to look at his stunned face. His wet lips stayed parted as he watched her, confused. Then he wrapped his arms around her and squeezed her to his chest. He kissed her back slowly, at first, like someone who knew what he was doing. His fingers tugged and tangled in her hair. When he touched her tongue with his, their soft kissing veered fast into deep desperation. As Quinn sank inside this endless kiss, she already ached for the next one.

The sliding door whooshed open. They jumped apart. Quinn stood panting quietly, damp and disoriented. Seth slipped back, away from the pool of light on the patio.

"Are you out here, Quinn?" Trish asked, squinting into the darkness. Quinn coughed into her hand as an excuse to wipe off her mouth.

"I'm here."

"The band is starting."

"Actually, I'm out. I don't feel so good. Stomachache."

Trish made a sympathetic face and motioned her inside. "Let me get your keys from Terrence. Is that your first beer?" she asked, motioning to Quinn's full cup on the patio. Quinn nodded.

"Thanks," she said, letting Trish shepherd her inside. She headed to the top of the stairs while Trish located Terrence. A minute later, Trish pressed her keys into her hand. "Are you sure you can get a ride?" Quinn asked her.

"No problem. Feel better."

Quinn had never felt better in her life.

She unlocked the front door of her house two hours ahead of curfew. As she headed upstairs to fantasize in peace, her mom waved hello from the dining room table.

"Jason called," she said. "I thought you were with him."

"Um. No." Quinn avoided eye contact.

Twenty minutes later, Jason swung Quinn's hand as they strolled around the block and then back to her house. He held on to it as they reached the front steps and sat down. Tight green buds all around them waited for some mysterious signal to let their lime-colored leaves explode. Quinn blurted it.

"I think we should break up."

"What?" Jason demanded. Tension thrummed like a magnetic barrier between them. "Did I do something?"

Yes. No. She nibbled the scruffy cuticle on her thumb.

"You were rude to that kid selling candy bars."

"You're breaking up with me because I wouldn't buy overpriced chocolate from a panhandler?" he laughed. "C'mon, Quinn. Lighten up." She could tell he'd already smoothed things over in his own mind. "I'm sorry if you thought I was too harsh. Okay?"

"No. It's not the chocolate. That's just an example. I don't think you get me." There was nothing more to say. She watched surprise and hurt register in Jason's eyes as her words finally sank in. Her own relief spread through her like a lifting headache.

"You're right," Jason said. "I don't." He vaulted down the steps and walked away.

Lincoln High's cafeteria tried hard to show school spirit with its red-and-black tables, chairs, and wall stencils. But the overpowering fluorescent lights sort of canceled out the earnest rah-rah by making everyone look like heroin addicts. The following Monday, Quinn walked in with a group of friends. Trish had the rest of them practically crying over one of her loud, embellished stories. She was retelling a classic: the one about her stepdad marching her fifteen-year-old brother to the front pew of the church on Sunday morning after finding him in their bushes covered in vomit.

As Quinn followed the others to the lunch line, she spotted Seth sitting at a table on her right. He met her eyes but didn't smile. It was like he was waiting.

"I know that you're genuinely nice. Even though you have a lot of friends, you make a point of saying hello to people like me."

"Hi, Seth," she said, feeling her chest and face get hot. The room seemed more crowded than usual. Seth held a thin sandwich. The tendons on the undersides of his tan wrists tensed and rose slightly when she spoke.

"Hi, Quinn." His lunch bag was a washed and crinkled bread bag. The mustard-yellow sandwich container resembled one that Quinn's mom had tossed a decade ago. A tiny apple core sat on top of the bread sack next to an unopened carton of chocolate milk. He caught her staring at his meal.

"Fiestadas today. Gross," he said, wrinkling his nose.

Quinn watched his full mouth make the words. It hit her that she should say something. "Right. Yuck." She smiled at him. Seth tipped up his chin at Quinn. He smiled back.

In the food line, Quinn plunked a plastic tray on the metal track in front of the steam counter. Fiestadas posed as Mexican pizza, but self-respecting Lincoln High students referred to the combination of analog cheese and four crumbles of ground beef as "shit on a shingle." Quinn wasn't hungry anyway. She frowned. She never lost her appetite, not unless she had stomach flu. She took a saucer of canned pears and a roll.

As she and Trish joined their friends at their regular table, Quinn saw Seth rise from his chair over in no man's land. He jammed his Tupperware back into the bread sack and jump-shot the apple core into the trash can as he left. His worn, soft jeans bagged. He was thin but solid, with a cute boy butt and narrow hips. Quinn could still feel the muscles in the arms that had pulled her to him.

Michelle from Mr. Levine's class—with freshly dyed black hair and cobalt blue lipstick—slowed down to say hi to Seth. He stopped briefly. He laughed at something she said. Apparently, Michelle played Janet most weekends at *The Rocky Horror Picture Show*. She'd probably never been boring a day in her life. Michelle touched Seth's arm while she told what must have been the rest of the story. Seth laughed, waving goodbye before walking out of sight. Quinn ached.

"We haven't had any big conversations, but I feel like I know you."

Trish had stopped talking. Quinn turned her head to pretend to listen again. Trish was watching her closely.

"What?" Quinn demanded.

Trish raised an eyebrow. Her bangs bristled today with effort and hairspray. She sucked the Cheetos dust off her fingers. Unpeeling the waxed paper square from a pat of butter suddenly required Quinn's full and immediate attention.

"We should talk," Trish finally said.

CHAPTER 12
SECOND-STRIKE CAPABILITY

Mr. Levine greeted Seth as he walked into class.

"Stop by soon," he said in a low voice. "I have those financial aid materials for you." Seth gave him a noncommittal nod. "Or give me a call sometime. You still have my number?"

"Thanks, I will," Seth said, but kept walking toward his desk.

Someone had traced a peace sign in the electromagnetic dust on the black filing cabinet near Mr. Levine's desk. Above it, it said, "Work For." Seth leaned in for a closer view. The artist had accidentally drawn the Mercedes logo, forgetting to include the extra line that should bisect the lower third of the circle. Seth smiled to himself.

Trish was running her fingers through her big hair. Michelle asked Seth to loan her a pen. Once he'd dropped his lunch tray in the cafeteria in front of God and everybody. Michelle had helped him clean it up without saying a word. She looked like she spent a lot of time not eating, but she was nice. They'd made out briefly behind the Super C last year. No sparks, but no hard feelings.

Mr. Levine walked over to his desk and peered into his empty coffee cup. He sighed and stretched his arms behind his back.

Seth heard the telltale sound of Pop Rocks pouring out of a candy box and sizzling as they mixed with someone's spit.

"Do you have enough of those to share with the class?" Mr. Levine asked the girl sitting behind Quinn.

"No. Sorry," the girl muttered. She wore thirty extra pounds like she wasn't afraid to take up some space. She turned and whispered something to Drew, who let out a big guffaw. Mr. Levine looked annoyed, like someone who'd spent his whole weekend painting a house. He walked over and got right in the girl's face.

"Would you please trade desks with Seth?"

The class went dead quiet. Seth felt Quinn watching him as he and the girl gathered their stuff and switched seats. He wished he knew what was going on in Quinn's head. Had Saturday night only been a hookup? Or had it been the start of something? He hadn't been able to read her at all at lunch. Now here he was having to sit at close range for an hour and smell her shampoo. Ilene turned and gave him a brief smile.

Mr. Levine kicked off Mondays with current-event reviews. A skinny guy in the back row reported on the thousands of Chinese college students marching for democracy.

"Can we support democracy in a communist country with a rotten human rights record without screwing up our relationship with the government? How do we advise President Bush? Seth?"

Why was Mr. Levine picking on him again? Jesus. And how was he supposed to concentrate when he could smell Quinn's hair?

"All I know is what he probably will do," Seth said.

"Which is?"

"Nothing much. Like Reagan in South Africa."

"Is there another way for America to support democracy besides using formal diplomacy?" Seth shrugged. Mr. Levine waited for someone else to respond. Seth tried to distract himself by looking outside.

A lone maple tree shook out last night's five-minute downpour like it could afford to be fast and loose with rain water, like a dry summer didn't loom mere days ahead. The electrical storm had flickered and blazed for an hour before letting go of barely a half inch of rain. Today's tropical steam felt like unfinished business.

Quinn was staring at her desk like she was begging to not be called on.

"What did we learn about ourselves in South Africa?" Mr. Levine demanded.

The room stilled. Seth finally saw what he meant.

"What's another powerful diplomatic tool besides having leaders in suits talk to leaders in suits?" Mr. Levine sounded vaguely irritated by the silence. "Quinn?"

Quinn cringed. Even a week ago, Seth would have enjoyed seeing her squirm, but not now. Now she felt to him like a lifeline. He didn't think. He knocked his pen off his desk so that it fell near Quinn's foot. As he reached for it, he cleared his throat.

"Citizen action," he whispered to her.

Quinn froze for a second, then tucked her hair behind her ear. "Citizen action?" she offered.

"Precisely," Mr. Levine beamed. "Thank you, Ambassador Ganey." He walked to the other side of the room, warming to the subject of test-driving "grassroots" foreign relations.

Quinn turned her head and caught Seth's eye for a nanosecond.

"Thanks," she whispered, still flushing. "You saved me."

After class, Seth yanked open his locker. He pulled out his calculus text and scraped its increasingly mushy corners on the sharp edge of the door. The school would probably fine him for that plus the super-adhesive "Dukakis for President" sticker he'd stuck on the back wall. He didn't care. He hitched up his Levi's and brushed his hair off his face. He added "get a haircut" to his mental list.

"Hi, Seth." He jumped as if he'd been bitten, crashing his locker closed. He spun to face Quinn. He watched her read his T-shirt, a cartoon nuclear mushroom cloud and comic script that said, "That's All, Folks!"

"Um. I broke up with Jason." She watched his face like she was waiting for a balloon to pop. A sharp line ran between her brows.

It hit him slowly: she was offering this as good news. Seth let out the breath he hadn't realized he'd been holding. His smile was a reflex, like a signal to himself that what he'd heard a second ago might turn out to be real. "This is a surprise," he said slowly.

Quinn cleared her throat and came up with a faltering smile of her own. "A good one?" she asked.

Seth grinned at her and leaned sideways against his locker. "Yeah. A very good one."

She leaned against the row of locker doors, too, grinning back.

He felt ridiculous just standing there, but he was incapable of doing anything but smiling and leaning.

"Maybe we could take a walk?" she asked.

"Yes." Brilliant.

"Meet you at the bleachers in maybe ten minutes?" Her natural coloring was making a comeback.

"Yes," he said, rolling his eyes at his own inarticulateness.

She liked it. "Okay." She pushed herself away from the locker and pantomimed wiping her forehead. "Bye." She gave him a little wave as she walked back down the hall.

"Bye." Seth waved back, following her with his eyes until she turned the corner. He opened his locker again and spent the next nine minutes staring into it, beaming like a fool.

Quinn sat on the lowest bench by the field where the track team was practicing. She quit chewing her cuticles when Seth walked up with his hands in his pockets. She gestured toward a paved street that ran south from the school.

"I'm on Sheridan," she said as they walked past the parking lots. "Walk me home?" He nodded. It figured that she lived on Sheridan Boulevard, a charming, winding mile of large old houses insulated by old-fashioned brick-paved side streets. It was kind of far away from school, though. She must have read his mind. "My parents open enrolled me here. My dad went to Lincoln High, more diversity, blah, blah. And they think it builds character for me to walk."

"Is it working?"

"It's hard to tell."

They both laughed sort of shakily as they cut across the cracking concrete boulevard and walked slowly up the side of Twenty-Fourth Street. Quinn's constant tucking and untucking of her hair gave Seth a small hit of courage.

"You surprised me," he said, pulling up his backpack.

A strand of Quinn's hair had caught on her earring. It made a shiny loop against her cheek. "Which time?"

Seth laughed. "Both."

"Yeah, well, after someone tells you you're smart, pretty, and genuine, it's hard to bounce back, you know?"

Seth smiled at his shoes. "I'm glad I waited almost three years to say anything."

"Yeah. Perfect timing. By the way, how was the band?"

"What band?" he joked. "Was there a band?" She giggled. "I left right after you did. I thought my cousin Lee was going to beat me up, but I wasn't in the mood."

"Wait, Lee? Tall guy in a plaid shirt?"

"Yeah. Did you meet him?"

"At the keg. He gave me a really weird look when Terrence introduced us."

"I may have mentioned you to him."

"Really? What did you say?"

"That I spilled my guts to you in a note, after which point you kicked my ass."

"I guess that about covers it." They walked a block in silence, then drifted across A Street's two-lane, late-afternoon traffic.

"I used to live near George Washington University," Seth said. "I bet you'll like it."

"You think?" Quinn kicked a chunk of gravel every few paces. Sweet freckles scattered over her nose and cheekbones. "I'm not so sure," she blurted a minute later. Her eyes widened as if she'd surprised herself, but she kept going. "I'm scared of almost everything. That I'll hate my roommate. That I'll be homesick. That I won't be able to keep up with the prep school geniuses."

Seth wanted to take her hand, but he stopped himself. First of all, they were in public. And second of all, he was a chickenshit. Seth put his hands back in his pockets.

"You'll be great. You'll fit right in," he said. "You should intern for President Bush while you're there."

Her laugh bubbled out of her as if someone had flipped an on switch. It didn't even build; it was like it was right there waiting for company. He laughed with her a little, taking in the contrast close-up between her extravagant giggle and her reserved blue eyes.

"I'll send you a postcard from the White House."

"Perfect." He pulled up his backpack again. It was too heavy to carry on just one shoulder, but only losers used both straps.

They crossed a busy street and walked into an older, more picturesque part of town. As they approached Sheridan Boulevard from mansion-packed Lake Street, Seth quietly took in the big houses and tidy lawns. So this was how the other five percent lived. Quinn fidgeted with her hair as they stopped in front of an ivy-covered Tudor-style house.

"There's no grass in your yard," Seth observed. Someone had landscaped the whole half of the yard to the left of the curved sidewalk. A forked woodchip path threaded toward the back of the house. In a couple of weeks, those spirea hedges between the Ganeys' property and their neighbors' to the south would probably bury their driveway in tiny white petals. His mom would think the Ganeys' garden had "good bones." She'd like the classy effect of soft evergreen shrubs anchoring beds of hosta, grasses, and white tulips.

"Dad hates mowing and won't hire someone," Quinn said as a tall, slim, frankly gorgeous blond woman in a blue dress and heels pulled open the front door. She stepped out and started to pull it closed before noticing them.

"Hi, honey! How was school? I'm off, okay? Who's your friend?" she called in one breath. The mother. Wow.

"Hi, Mom," Quinn said. "This is Seth. We have a class together."

"Hi, Seth." Mrs. Ganey smiled. He saw her take in his threadbare jeans and mushroom cloud T-shirt. Shit.

"Hi, Mrs. Ganey."

She batted away his greeting. "God, please call me Evelyn."

"Okay." No way would he call her Evelyn.

Mrs. Ganey turned to Quinn. "I have a meeting, but Dad's home early. He'll make eggs unless you have a better idea."

Seth and Quinn stood at the end of the sidewalk and watched her mom drive away in a Volvo. Quinn rolled her eyes and smiled before picking up their conversation.

"So, what are you doing next year?" she asked him.

Seth felt his neck muscles tighten. "I'll work at the lumberyard full-time."

"The one by school?"

He didn't hear any judgment in her voice. "Yeah. Right now, I stock shelves. But they're teaching me to drive a forklift." He sneaked a sideways glance. "Mr. Levine wants me to apply to colleges." Where had that come from? He wanted to grab the words and stuff them back in his mouth.

"For next year?" Quinn asked.

"No. I don't know. It's complicated." His mom would need him around more—not less—in the near future. He didn't think there was any way he could add classes to a full-time work schedule. And asking his mom about it would only make her feel guiltier than she already did. The last thing either of them needed right now was for him to tip their shaky balance.

Quinn waited for him to keep going. He didn't. She'd ripped off his comfortable disguise and didn't even know it.

CHAPTER 13
SUPERPOWERS

"I can give you a ride," Quinn said. "Unless you'd rather meet my dad first."

Seth's unfamiliar laugh was low and easy. "Ride sounds good."

Quinn had avoided her dad since their argument. She still felt humiliated that she'd argued with her feelings again instead of her brain. This morning, she'd asked him some friendly questions about gardening. He'd acted polite but stiff, like he couldn't quite place her.

She and Seth walked in silence up the brick driveway to the garage. Quinn's chest clanged like she'd been sprung from a racing gate. Being alone with Seth in her dad's car made her a whole new layer of nervous. She fastened her seatbelt and adjusted the vents. She forgot to look back as she reversed out of the driveway.

Quinn watched Seth sideways. He sank back into the cushy seat. He smiled to himself as he rubbed the leather upholstery under his knees. As she watched him, something eased inside Quinn like she'd peeled off a too-tight jacket. They approached South Street.

"Where am I going?" she asked. Seth pointed her east.

"We live really close to school."

"Do you have a big family?"

"It's just me and my mom. I'll introduce you sometime."

"I'd love to meet her."

"I didn't mean today," he said, instantly serious. He gazed out at the South Branch Library.

"No, I know," she said, turning left at the arrow. It was like she'd accidentally stepped in something.

"She doesn't like surprises." Seth was still staring out the window as the tidiness of Quinn's neighborhood gave way to gas stations and peeling houses. "She has MS. She's in a wheelchair. I take care of her."

Quinn thought of Trish's uncle Matt, coughing and shivering through the final stages of AIDS. Trish's mom took care of him some evenings. She always cried when she came home. Quinn had nothing to offer up to that kind of bleakness.

"I'm sorry," she said. As they veered left, the solemn intro to a Madonna song spilled into their silence.

"Man, I fuckin' hate this song!" Seth said, curing Quinn's pity in one sentence. He smiled an immediate, head-shaking apology, which made her laugh.

They passed the high school and turned on a nearby side street. The sagging old houses in Seth's neighborhood clashed with 1970s-style apartment buildings: big blocks of cement whose low front windows made them look like they'd been built on quicksand.

"Here it is," Seth said, gesturing to a tiny beige bungalow.

They stopped. The crumbling steps of Seth's house led up to a sloping slab that posed as a porch and a flimsy aluminum storm door.

A neighbor was raking his lawn across the street. He squinted at the car before recognizing and waving at Seth. Seth waved back to their audience.

"Damn," he said. "I really, really want to kiss you right now."

Quinn nodded. She shifted the car into neutral, but all she wanted was for them to be alone, to race back to the dark patio at Terrence's house. She smiled.

"You can kiss me telepathically."

"With tongue?"

Quinn blushed. She swatted his chest. "And biceps."

Now he was the one blushing. "I like where you're going with this."

"We're getting good at sneaking around."

Seth nodded. "We're extremely mysterious."

"What did Lee say when you told him about us?"

"I didn't tell him anything."

"Because we're so mysterious."

"Right. Wanna sneak around with me on Friday?"

"Definitely."

He took her hand off the gearshift, squeezing it with rough fingers. "That's our super-secret handshake." He gave her one last smile before climbing out and shutting the door.

On the drive home, she turned up the volume on "Like a Prayer," her favorite song. She shouted the words to vent the anxiety of the world's scariest, best day. Trish had mixed this tape for her, recording this song four times.

Quinn's chest tightened as the song wound down at a stop-light. Trish didn't like Seth. And she wasn't the type to sugarcoat her opinions for anyone's sake. That gave Quinn and Seth one more reason to sneak around.

CHAPTER 14
ZONES OF OCCUPATION

Seth climbed the marble steps in the main part of the school. He held on to the shellacked wood railing at the top step, waiting for the tsunami of someone's Polo cologne to blow by and let him breathe again before he rounded the corner. He grinned at his shoes; yesterday he'd gotten the girl. Now he was casually walking by the girl's locker before class.

Quinn's face lit up when she saw him. That felt like getting ten years' worth of birthday presents. Seth made sure no one was looking before he winked at her. She giggled into the backpack she was stuffing. She bumped her locker door with her hip. Seth could watch her do that all day, he thought as he kept walking. He could watch her do anything all day.

Three days later, they piled their plates full of pizza at Valentino's. She pulled a pepperoni slice from under a mountain of spinach pasta salad. The girl could eat. Seth tried hard not to stare at her lips.

After dinner, they walked along the south edge of the university campus. As they approached the Sheldon Gallery's grassy sculpture garden, Seth reached for Quinn's hand. He squeezed it gently. She squeezed back. He stared straight ahead to hide the dorky smile on his face. In the six days since neither of them heard Green Day perform, Seth felt like he'd been impersonating a regular person. All he could think about was kissing her.

They paused in front of a huge black metal geometric figure. It looked like the distorted body of the big red dog in the book he'd loved as a kid. It was as though it wanted to lumber over to its bowl of kibble, if only it weren't missing its head and a leg. Seth leaned in to read the plaque: *Willy* by Tony Smith.

"*Willy?*" Seth said. "More like Clifford."

Quinn laughed. The "feet" on Willy begged to be sat on. Seth wasn't sure, though, if you were allowed to sit on an outdoor sculpture.

"Can we sit here?" Quinn asked him, gesturing to Willy's "foot." Seth sat down and pulled her next to him, wiping his other sweaty palm on his faded but freshly washed Levi's. A sweet-smelling breeze blew through the sculpture garden in little gusts. Quinn smelled like shampoo that a drugstore didn't sell and the apple pizza they'd eaten for dessert. Her lip gloss had worn off.

Seth needed to kiss those bare lips. She turned to say something to him and found him staring at her mouth. Since it wasn't pitch-dark this time, he lost his nerve and looked away. But Quinn's warm hand reached out and touched his jaw, gently forcing him to face her again. When she put her hand back into her lap, he grabbed it, lacing their fingers together. He leaned in, pressing his lips against hers. They were soft and warm. When she kissed him back, her parted lips gave him an instant hard-on. Seth touched her top lip with his tongue. Her soft gasp made him feel like a rock star. He shivered when she reached her hand around the back of his neck and pulled him closer. They kissed until his lips were numb. They missed the movie.

Seth needed to get home; his mom would worry. As the sun set, they walked by a naked bronze woman sitting inside the thick outlines of a bronze box. Her foot pushed against one of the walls that crushed in on her.

"I know just how she feels," Seth said.

CHAPTER 15
ROLLBACK

Quinn ran late to every class the next Monday. She stood at her locker, trying to remember her combination. Trish approached from the direction of the girls' bathroom. Quinn got ready to tell her about Jason and deal with the hazing about losing her mind that would definitely follow.

Trish rushed up and shoved a notebook into Quinn's arms; she'd borrowed it after the South Africa lecture.

"Thanks, O Goddess of Thorough Note-Taking. Mr. Levine lost me after Manifest Destiny," she said.

Quinn scowled. Leave it to Trish to slack off and then ridicule her best friend for taking notes and bailing her out.

"You're welcome," Quinn said pointedly. She checked her reflection in her magnetic locker mirror. The overhead hallway lights made her whole face look smudged. She had to hip bump her locker twice to make it latch.

"Do you know what I think?" Trish asked, ignoring Quinn's sarcasm and striding with her toward seventh period. "I think Seth Burton likes you."

"I doubt it," Quinn said a little too forcefully. Trish waited.

Quinn spun out a more careful answer. "I'm sure if he thinks of me at all, it's as a prissy conservative circus freak or something," she said as casually as possible. "Besides," she asked, smiling, "Isn't he your boyfriend?"

"No." Trish shook her head slowly and smiled. "He likes you. I see him check you out in class. Whadayasay, Quinn?" She dug her elbow into Quinn's ribs. It hurt. "You could take him to prom in that Springsteen T-shirt he wears every day."

"You don't have to be mean," Quinn said quietly as they passed through the hallway doors. She didn't feel like sprinting today.

"I'm only teasing. God, lighten up." Trish's pace slowed as she looked at Quinn's profile.

"What?" Quinn asked. A guy shoved past her and almost knocked her off balance.

"Nothing," Trish finally said.

Quinn slid into her desk a minute later as the bell rang. She gave a little wave to Ilene, who waved back. Mr. Levine dug through a drawer in an overstuffed filing cabinet, oblivious to the classroom. Quinn felt Ilene watching her aggressive notebook page flipping. Her expression asked the question.

"Jason and I broke up," Quinn blurted in a low voice. Ilene waited for details. "All of a sudden, I felt invisible, you know?" Ilene, though she'd never come right out and said it, wasn't a Jason fan. "I spent five months thinking he was amazing. I'm just now catching on to the fact that he's spent the last five months thinking the same thing."

Ilene laughed. She leaned over and squeezed Quinn's wrist. "'Just say no' to squirrely debaters," she said.

"Why didn't you let me talk you out of it?" Trish demanded that afternoon as she rummaged for junk food in her mom and stepdad's gleaming white kitchen. The matching magnets on the refrigerator held Trish's littlest brother's artwork at perfect square angles.

"I didn't want you to talk me out of it, that's why. And I was worried I might let you." Trish's bluntness sometimes made Quinn nervous, but it also freed her up to be blunt herself. "Maybe him being adorable doesn't make up for the fact that he's kind of selfish. And he talks down to me lately, like I'm not quite good enough for him. And if that's how he's going to treat me, then he's not good enough for me." She swallowed hard. "Okay?"

Trish found an open pack of Twizzlers at the back of a drawer. She pulled off the Chip Clip and pulled out a stuck-together bunch of red licorice. As she yanked the strips apart, she looked hard at Quinn for a few seconds, as if making sure her eyes and words matched.

"Okay." Trish passed her a twisted column of licorice.

"Maybe that makes me selfish, too."

"No. You're a total pain in the ass, for sure," Trish said, "but you're one of the least selfish people I've ever met."

Quinn's gut loosened like she'd unfastened the top button of her skirt after Thanksgiving dinner. "Thanks, I think."

"I'm sorry for not paying closer attention. I didn't know how it was with Jason."

"It's okay." Quinn meant it. "I didn't know either until lately. I mean, I knew it, but I was trying not to know it."

"If Jason thought you weren't good enough, then he's a jerk.

I'm putting him at the top of my shit list."

"Maybe you should pay off your fashion violation first," Quinn said, picking a puffy Teenage Mutant Ninja Turtles sticker off Trish's jeans.

"Thanks," Trish said, cementing the sticker to the bottom of the spice cupboard. She put two nubs of licorice under her top lip and leered at Quinn with red candy fangs. "Sun porch or my room? I have new CDs."

"Your room." Quinn followed Trish, smiling at how her friend kicked out her suede ankle boots to the sides as she walked, like someone who was maximizing her spatial impact. On anyone else, that cutoff T-shirt would be absurd. On Trish, it looked fearless.

When Trish dropped her off at home that evening, her parents were watching basketball in the basement family room.

"Hustle, hustle!" Quinn's dad shouted at the Seton Hall defense. Her parents hardly ever sat in front of the television, let alone on a Monday night. They had views about television: it was only for morons unless they, themselves, wanted to catch Letterman or get a video from Blockbuster. Her dad had given up on programming the VCR and had covered its flashing numbers with a square of gray duct tape.

Her mom said hello before scowling back down at her endless fuzzy knitting project from hell. The NCAA championship game was a nail-biter. At the half, her dad flopped back in his seat as if exhausted and saw Quinn sitting cross-legged in the corduroy beanbag on the floor.

"Hullo there," he said, standing up during a commercial. "I'm getting a beer. Do either of you need anything?" He smiled at

Quinn. A real one, not one of those tight ones she'd been getting since that day on the deck.

"I broke up with Jason," Quinn said.

Her mom stopped knitting. She measured Quinn for a minute with her eyes but seemed satisfied enough to go back to her project. Her dad took the information for what it was: a peace offering. He sat back down.

"Did you argue about something?" he asked.

"No. He kind of made me feel . . . lonely." The muted television now showed a big-breasted blond eating a chocolate bar.

Her dad pressed his fingertips together in front of his face. "It's funny how the wrong person can make you feel worried and insecure. But being with the right person can make you feel like you love yourself as much as you love them. You feel happy and confident, generous and smart."

He headed upstairs to get his beer. Quinn and her mom shared a conspiratorial eye roll.

"Seth seems nice," her mom said casually.

Quinn made her face pretend that this remark was totally random. She shrugged. "He is nice. Just a friend, though."

"Mm . . . ," her mom murmured into her knitting. Lightning flickered outside, making the television reception flicker, too.

Whatever. Quinn sank back into the beanbag, wondering if Seth was watching Michigan beat Seton Hall in overtime.

CHAPTER 16
ESCALATION

The following Friday, after a stop at Goodrich Dairy, Seth and Quinn walked through the dense spruce- and pine-lined paths at Pioneers Park. They sipped their milkshakes. At the duck pond, they paused at what looked like four crumbling Grecian columns. Quinn pointed to the clump of yellow flowers at the base of one of them.

"Aren't those cute?" she asked.

Seth's mom would call those weeds. He stirred his milk shake. "They're wild primroses," he said. Her look said that he knew way too much about flowers for a guy. He shrugged. According to the bronze plaque, the sandstone had been quarried in Virginia in the early 1800s and used to build the federal treasury in Washington, DC. President Lincoln had stood between these actual columns to view the troops during the Civil War. "Proving again that the coolest things in Nebraska came from Virginia," Seth said before taking a swig of his melting drink.

"You keep telling yourself that," Quinn said as she turned back to the path.

Seth grabbed her hand and reeled her in. He kissed her milk-shake-cold mouth. He liked kissing her standing up; he had a three-inch height advantage. Who was he kidding? He liked kissing her in any position. A minute later they heard little kids' voices. They broke apart and headed back up the hill.

"About five years ago," Quinn told him, "my family stayed with friends in Kansas City." They sat now clasping their knees at the top of the park's wooden sledding ramp—the steep side. "I snooped in a drawer in their family room, found a porn video, took it home, and watched it."

Seth hoped she didn't have superhuman expectations of mere high school guys. He hoped for a lot of things. "And?"

"And it was interesting. But only for about five minutes. The people were like robots."

Seth wondered if girls had any idea how often the average guy thought about sex, how little it mattered if porn was "interesting" or not. "I didn't actually have you pegged as a porn connoisseur."

"Yeah, well, as you know, I'm very deep and mysterious."

Seth stretched his arms over his head. Everything about this sprawling park made him happy: the long sloping hill, the twilight view of prairie grass and pine trees, this girl who kept surprising him. It was like the horizon was reassuring him that anything was possible.

"I steal a pack of Hostess Ho Hos every time I go to the Super C," he said. "I'm like a modern-day Robin Hood."

"A real hero," Quinn agreed. She lowered her voice. "I smoke about a pack a month of my dad's cigarettes."

"Gross," Seth said.

"I know. A girl's gotta have a vice, though, you know?"

"I tried pot at a party a few years ago," Seth said. "I coughed so hard I threw up. My cousin Lee had to take me home." Seth picked at the shiny wooden planks, worn soft by decades of tobogganers. They released a sun-bleached chemical whiff of creosote.

"Lee and his friends must have thought you were incredibly cool."

"Extremely."

"Green Day can probably hold their pot." He laughed. The band had named itself after marijuana.

"If I had a time machine," Quinn said, "I'd fast-forward through next year and that horrible feeling of starting over and feeling clueless."

"My life is defined by starting over and feeling clueless," Seth said. "I'd use my time machine to rewind to two years ago and ask you out in sophomore English."

"What if I'd said no? You were probably a whiny Democrat even then."

"You would have said no—and not only because I was a whiny Democrat. I had major hygiene issues then." Seth smiled. "But you would have come crawling back two years sooner."

"You liked that, didn't you? The crawling back part."

"Goddamn right." He put his arm around her and squeezed. "I rarely get to see a Republican grovel." Quinn reached for his hand and rubbed the underside of his wrist with one finger, sending goose bumps to the back of his neck.

He turned and kissed her. Quinn relaxed against him, kissing him back. She teased him with her tongue, slowly licking the corners of his mouth and sucking his upper lip. She pressed the hand he'd draped over her shoulder against her breast.

Seth groaned. His hard-on strained against his jeans. He used the four brain cells he had left to think about slowing down before things got out of hand. But she didn't act like she wanted him to stop. As his left hand crept under her shirt, she turned to face him. This was too easy, too amazing. He slipped his hand under her bra, copping a skin-on-skin feel for the first time in his life. Her breast was round, heavy. The tits on girls in porn magazines looked like cantaloupes. (Not that their inflated appearance interfered in the least with his whacking off.) Quinn's were soft, though, and squishy except for the nipple, which got rock hard under his thumb. Her breathing got harder, too.

When she finally pulled away, he felt suffocated by the lack of her.

Seth leaned back on his elbows and closed his eyes. He could smell lilac bushes from all the way up here. As Quinn tucked herself back in, he turned around to look at Lincoln's tiny skyline in the dusk. From the chipped black metal rails of the sledding ramp, the park's architect had offered them a perfect view of the phallic-shaped State Capitol. It really did deserve all the jokes. But Penis of the Prairie or not, the tall, gold-domed building looked especially art deco and imposing in the twilight.

The sky faded and stretched into cottony strands. They listened to the crickets until a beat-up blue Ford Pinto squealed into the parking lot below. They heard whoops of male laughter as beer bottles hit the pavement.

"I hate big parties," Quinn said. "They make me nervous."

Seth agreed. "I'd rather eat razor blades. And talking in front of people makes me want to puke."

"Me, too."

"This from the debate queen?"

"My dad said debating would help."

"And?"

"It didn't." The absurdity of spending two years doing something she hated seemed to hit her then. She laughed, each syllable gliding up and down a soft musical scale. Listening to her was like lying under the down comforter on his aunt's spare bed, insulated from everything that wasn't safe and warm.

"You should see Ilene doing her first negative rebuttal. She goes into this head zone and completely obliterates the other team's argument. Me? I'm pitting out my blazer before we even start."

Now Seth laughed. He fiddled with the shoestring on his high-tops. He found a new topic. "If I were rich, I'd sign up Drew for about fifty of those CD-of-the-month clubs that they have in the Sunday ads. Easy listening and country western, I think. They'd mail him about ten a day."

"That's utterly brilliant," Quinn said.

Seth felt brilliant. For once his real life was living up to his fantasy life. Okay, almost. But this was starting to feel real, like it was actually him surrounded by starry skies and moist air and sitting next to the girl he loved. The girl he loved. He breathed out slowly.

"True confessions?" he asked. Quinn nodded. "I took the ACT. Mr. Levine made me do it while I still remembered the material from my classes. I saved some money from each paycheck and sent it in. I got off work, took the test, intercepted the mail, and never told my mom. I got a thirty."

Quinn smiled down at her own shoes before pushing him over from a sitting position to a sprawling one.

"Me, too. I got a thirty, too," she said. Seth laughed. This was so easy. "If I could do whatever I wanted," Quinn said, "I'd take a year or two off before college and go to Europe and India. I'd take trains all over and go three days without a shower and stay in youth hostels and take cooking classes. I'd do moronically inappropriate things before getting on with my boring, responsible life."

"I'll go with you." Seth liked the idea of making plans, any plans. Maybe he'd travel someday. A flock of ducks flew in a loose *W* formation over the tops of the pine trees at the bottom of the hill. "I'll move back to DC and go to GW with you." This ridiculous daydream actually felt more real at this moment than the life he led. He really could move to DC. He'd show her his old apartment and his basketball hoop, the monuments and museums. Quinn made him want to do more, to be more. He offered up an even bigger secret. "If I were rich, I'd hire a full-time nurse for my mom and go to college." He stared straight ahead, releasing his breath slowly. Someone who was going to college herself wouldn't think he was a hypocrite for trying to climb up a rung. She stroked his tight knuckles.

"What about going part-time?" she asked.

His body tensed. He'd only wanted to extend the daydream—not invite her to fix his life. "On whose dime?" She didn't seem clued into the fact that he lived on Social Security with his mom who was dying a slow, ugly death.

"Grants? Scholarships? There's money out there."

"Mr. Levine says that, too, but no one wants to give money to a part-time student."

"Have you asked?" She made it sound simple.

"Quinn, you don't get it. Even if I got in somewhere—and even if I got a scholarship—I probably wouldn't be able to finish. My mom is really sick. And quitting halfway and knowing what I was missing would be way worse than not going at all."

Quinn scrunched up her forehead. She plunged on, oblivious to his warning signs. "What does your mom think?" Seth didn't say anything. "I mean, going to college wouldn't take any more time away from her than going to high school."

Seth pressed his lips together, trying to think of a way to make Quinn understand without hurting her feelings. She didn't know the first thing about the loyalty, heartbreak, and resentment a guy shared with his single mother, let alone his sick single mother.

"I have to start working full-time after graduation. And Mom's MS will just keep getting worse. Her legs are starting to feel numb. She needs a brace sometimes just to stand up. She pees her pants. She can't hold stuff. And I'm the one who takes care of her."

"I know." Quinn sounded impatient. "I'm only saying that you might graduate sooner if you start sooner."

"I know you think my mom controls my life or something, but she doesn't. Her MS controls us both. This sucks for me, okay?" His voice sounded loud in the stillness. Quinn's silence, though, didn't concede anything. Seth pulled his arm away from her. "You have no fucking idea. What do you know about making hard choices, huh? The biggest decision you've ever had to make was picking George Washington over Boston U."

Maybe he should have felt guilty when Quinn shrank back from him and blinked back tears. But what he did feel was pure fury. How had this conversation crashed and burned so fast? For a few minutes, he'd felt safe. He'd felt almost free.

CHAPTER 17
FALLOUT

Quinn finally came out of the movie theater restroom. She'd been bawling her eyes out for a full ten minutes after seeing *Field of Dreams.* She'd assumed they'd catch *Major League* or some other guy film, but like the idiot she'd confirmed herself to be this morning, she'd let Seth talk her into a Saturday matinee of one that she'd already known had an emotional ending. It had been a week since their argument at the park. Taking him to a movie was the rest of her apology for getting in his business. They were trying to get back to normal.

Someone was waving and smiling at her from the concession stand. Quinn blinked her swollen eyelids a few times. It was Ilene, standing in line next to her boyfriend, Caleb. Now Ilene frowned at Quinn. She came over and checked out Quinn's streaked face. Ilene took her arm and led her to an empty bench under a *Batman* poster near a window.

"*Field of Dreams*, right?" she asked. "Should I demand a refund?"

Quinn searched the lobby but didn't see Seth. She started crying again, her tears and snot now outpacing her miserable swipes with the backs of her hands. Ilene stepped sideways to shield Quinn from the crowded lobby.

"Take your time," Ilene said. As Quinn started to calm down, Ilene ducked under the velvet rope surrounding the concessions island. Quinn watched her pinch a bunch of napkins from the dispenser, pointedly ignoring the grumpy balding man with the "Manager" nametag. When she came back, Quinn blew her nose on the napkins and let Ilene pull her closer to the exit doors by the video games.

"I'm pregnant," Quinn whispered.

"What?" Ilene's eyes swerved to Quinn's face.

"I'm pregnant," she said again as Seth appeared next to Ilene. Quinn jumped a little. Two seconds screeched into slow motion as she met his stricken eyes. He'd heard. He offered her a tiny, sympathetic smile. Then he gestured feebly that he'd wait for her outside. He walked away.

"Jesus Christ," Ilene breathed. Quinn stared out the window and answered Ilene's unasked questions in a flat voice.

"We used condoms. I don't know what happened. This morning, I peed on every test at Walgreens."

Ilene rubbed Quinn's movie-chilled upper arm. She stared at the 1970s carpet. "What does Jason think?" she finally asked.

"I only realized yesterday that I hadn't gotten my period. I haven't told him."

"But you're going to?"

Quinn hadn't actually considered it. Not that she'd had much time to consider anything.

"No. I don't think I will." Ilene waited. "It's not like he'd feel some fatherly attachment or want me to have it," Quinn said. "Nothing would piss him off more, actually, than to think something might interfere with his master plan." As she said this out loud, she knew it was true.

"But don't you think he deserves to know?" Ilene asked.

Quinn picked at the fraying hole in the knee of her jeans. She looked into Ilene's concerned face. "No, actually. I don't. Even thinking about dealing with his ego one more time right now makes me want to scream."

Ilene nodded. She disagreed with her, Quinn could tell.

"You'll get an abortion?" Ilene asked.

Quinn's stomach knotted. Even the word itself—the onomatopoeia of it—had scary edges. "Yes."

Ilene waited.

"You think it's wrong," Quinn said.

"No . . . I . . ."

"It's so stupid—that whole 'when does life begin?' discussion. Like it's not totally obvious to everyone that if you don't kill it now it would become a baby. Why pretend?"

"I don't think it's wrong," Ilene said firmly.

"Really?"

"No."

"I love kids," Quinn said. "I want kids someday."

"Me, too."

"I just feel dumb, you know?" Quinn tucked her hair behind her ears and pulled on the ends. "Dumb for getting pregnant. Dumb because two days ago, I would have said that this only happens to sluts and stupid people. Remember Brandy Howell in gym class practically bragging about her abortion?" Ilene nodded. "And what about Theresa O'Brien last year, waddling through the hallways eating Hot Tamales?"

"A cautionary tale in Goodwill maternity clothes," Ilene agreed. "But, Quinn," she said, getting serious again. "Just because those girls aren't smart or ambitious or whatever doesn't mean they deserved to go through that."

"I didn't say they did."

"Mm . . ."

"Here comes Caleb," Quinn said, spying him across the lobby.

"What are you doing tonight?" Ilene asked quickly.

Quinn managed an ironic half smile. "Not much besides slitting my wrists."

"Pancakes later?"

Pure relief surged through Quinn's veins.

Seth squeezed her hand during the silent drive home.

He hugged her across the armrest when they reached his house. His Pink Floyd *The Wall* T-shirt gave off a comforting, clean-laundry smell.

"Please don't tell anyone, okay?" she asked him.

He shook his head at her. "Why would I tell anyone?" he asked, swatting her leg. "I like you."

Quinn smiled. "I like you, too."

"I'm still kind of mad at you, though. For last weekend, I mean."

Quinn nodded. She got it. "I know. I'm sorry. Clearly I'm in no position to tell anyone what choices to make."

Seth grinned. "You said it, not me." She allowed herself a smile. "I'm not going anywhere," he said. "Know that, okay?" Now Quinn started to cry again. She tried to get a grip. "Not that it's any of my business," Seth asked, "but what are you going to do?"

"Get an abortion. I just have to call and schedule it."

He nodded. "If you want, I'll come with you."

Quinn let the tears spill again now. She kicked herself—for the hundredth time in the past twenty-four hours—for wasting her virginity on the wrong guy. She leaned over and kissed the right one.

"I know *awkward* doesn't begin to cover this whole mess, but having you there would be great."

Three hours later, Quinn and Ilene waited for signs of a waitress in their faux leather booth. They agreed that the orange-and-teal decor in Lincoln's premier pancake house was the ugliest color combination ever conceived.

"Speaking of conceived." Ilene wiggled her ears at Quinn. They both laughed. "I blew off Caleb this afternoon and did some research at the library."

"You did? For me?" Quinn asked.

Ilene smiled. "I'm not in varsity forensics for nothing, you know."

"Ha-ha. So am I. You know what I did this afternoon? I took a nap."

"Has your mom noticed anything?"

"I don't think so."

"Are you going to tell her?"

"I want to. But I really don't want to. I have to, though, don't I? I'm only seventeen."

"Right. The Nebraska Unicameral, in its infinite wisdom, deems that you are old enough to be a mother, but not old enough to decide on your own to have an abortion. You'd have to get a lawyer and a judicial bypass."

Quinn fidgeted like a child sitting at the grown-ups' table. She'd read a recent headline about an abortion case going to the Supreme Court, but she didn't think it had to do with minors.

"What'll it be, girls?" The unsmiling waitress looked at least six months pregnant and reeked of cigarette smoke. Quinn and Ilene avoided each other's eyes as she poured their coffee. They ordered their pancakes and sausage.

"Remind me what a judicial bypass is?" Quinn asked. In theory, it sounded appropriate for a girl's parents to know about their kid's surgery. But Ilene was right about the irony; it was easier to become a teen mother than it was to get a learner's permit.

"If—for whatever reason—you can't ask for or get your parents' permission," Ilene said, "you convince a judge that you can decide for yourself. I called a lawyer . . . this"—she dug in her teeny pocketbook for a slip of paper—"Diane Jacobs. She could go with you. You'd have to spill your guts to a judge you've never met who may or may not decide that you're mature enough to get an abortion without your parents' permission."

"Are you serious?" Quinn flopped back against the fake leather seat. "That's so patronizing. I have my shit together way more than some adults I know."

"Un-fucking-believable." Ilene nodded.

Quinn tucked her hair behind her ears. Then, she untucked it. Having the actual surgery sounded easy compared to the stress of getting it set up. She either had to confide in a stranger or admit to her parents that she had had sex without a backup method of birth control. So much for thinking politics didn't affect her personally. She bent the tines of a fork backward as Ilene studied the sticky pie menu.

"So if I go for the judicial bypass, what happens after I dazzle the man in the black robe and he deigns to let me have an abortion?" Quinn added four sugars to her mug of coffee.

"You make an appointment at the clinic in Omaha, take the piece of paper he signs, and come up with two hundred and fifty dollars. Then you get a ride, have the abortion, take your Advil, and lie low for a couple of days without your parents catching on."

The tines of Quinn's fork now bent in alternating directions. "How do you know all this?"

"I told you. I went to the library." Ilene smiled. She didn't get into Harvard for nothing.

Back at home that night, Quinn called her sister. As she waited for Sarah to pick up the receiver, she tied a knot in the dangling loop of phone cord.

"Hello?" Sarah said.

"It's me," said Quinn. "I'm a mess."

"Define mess."

"Pregnant. Getting an abortion," Quinn said. She listened to a five-second silence.

"Oh, Quinn. Yep. That's definitely a mess." Sarah's voice

sounded uncharacteristically gentle. "Did Mom flip out?"

"I haven't told her. I can't decide if it would be worse to see her disappointment or if I should get a judicial bypass."

"How long does that take?

"A week or two, I think. Ilene says I can't even schedule the appointment until after get the piece of paper. But I don't think I can wait two more weeks. I want it out."

"You'll have to tell Mom, then." Sarah was right.

"I'd rather set my hair on fire."

"That's an option." Quinn could hear Sarah grinning through the phone. "At least you wouldn't need a judicial bypass."

The next morning, Quinn walked downstairs and pulled out a chair at the cluttered dining room table. She'd crossed an invisible threshold into a whole new echelon of nervous. Her hands were freezing and sweating at the same time. Even her vision blurred around the edges. She waited for her mom to stop writing.

"Where's Dad?" Quinn asked.

Her mom sipped her cold coffee. "Making another run to the nursery. Something about peat moss?" she said as she poked at a stack of mail.

"I have to talk to you." Quinn's voice wobbled. Her mom turned to offer her full attention. Quinn took a huge breath. "I'm pregnant."

Her mom put down her ballpoint pen. She stared at her. Quinn watched twenty different emotions flicker across her face. It made her feel like one of those fluffy milkweed seeds that floated around in late summer without ever finding the ground.

"Jesus Christ, Quinn," her mom finally blurted. "I don't know what to say." Quinn waited. "I didn't know you were having sex."

"Only a few times."

"Didn't you use birth control?"

"Of course we did, Mom! I'm not a total moron!" Quinn stopped herself. Her mom was right to be mad. "The condom must have ripped or something."

There were tears in her mom's brown eyes. "Okay," her mom said, mostly to herself. "Okay." She put her hand on Quinn's. "I'm shocked. I am." A minute ticked by as her mom fought her tears. She finally let them roll before wiping them away with the sleeve of her robe. "Okay. I'll help you. What do you need?" Her words felt like shelter, like ballast.

Quinn felt tears of relief seep down her face. "Please don't tell Dad," Quinn said. "At least for now."

Her mom rolled a pen back and forth on the table for a full thirty seconds. "You're putting me in a difficult position, Quinn. But for now, okay."

"And drive me and Seth to the abortion clinic." Quinn watched her mom's shoulders drop an inch.

"You've decided then."

"Yes."

Her mom closed her eyes and fanned herself with her hand. "Whew. I'm glad." Quinn smiled. "The one in Omaha?"

"Right."

"How much does it cost?"

"Two hundred fifty dollars. I only have half, but I can pay you back. I'm going to get a job this summer."

"Really? Where?"

Quinn shrugged. "Dunno. Maybe selling peat moss?"

Her mom smiled briefly. "How do you feel?"

"Nervous. And sort of tired."

Her mom nodded. "I remember the tired part." Then she stared hard at Quinn. "Honey, I know this feels awful right now. But it's going to be okay."

Now Quinn let her tears roll. She accepted her mom's hug, breathing in her coffee-smelling warmth.

CHAPTER 18
HOSTILE COMBATANTS

H er mom drove. Quinn watched vague pity register on her face when they stopped in front of Seth's house. But she barely acknowledged him when he scooted into the backseat.

The three of them rode in complete silence through Lincoln's small downtown and onto the interstate ramp. The flat sky against flat land disoriented Quinn, making her glad she wasn't driving. Seth paged through a magazine and occasionally squeezed her upper arm through the space between the seat and the window. Quinn waited for her mom or Seth to start a conversation. They didn't. It was like every minute added another pebble to their shaky pile of stress and nerves. Seth sneezed.

"Bless you," her mom said reflexively.

"Thanks," said Seth.

Silence enveloped them again. They passed wind-crippled trees and collapsed barns. Long rows of corn seedlings straightened and then disappeared as they sped by another field.

"Is the corn ever actually 'knee-high by the Fourth of July'?" Seth asked.

Quinn gestured with her chin to the field speeding by. "That's milo."

"Milo? What's that?

"Feed grain for cows."

"Why do you know about milo?" he asked.

Quinn shrugged.

None of them spoke again for a half hour. As they approached Omaha, the car crested hill after shallow hill as if it, too, rode a wave of fear.

"Seth," her mom finally said.

"Yes?"

"I'm not happy about the fact that my daughter is pregnant and having to get an abortion."

Quinn turned to her. "Wait, Mom—"

"No! I get to say this! I'm so angry! Seth, you seem like a smart kid. And I know Quinn is. You both should have been more careful."

"Mom!" Quinn shouted.

"What?" her mom shouted back.

"It's not Seth's," Quinn said softly.

Her mom tapped the brake. She signaled, pulling the car to a stop on the gravel edge of the highway. She glanced at Seth in the backseat before turning back to her. Quinn watched her jaw clench and unclench before she spoke.

"Are you telling me that you've had sex with two boys?"

Wow. Thanks for that, Mom, Quinn thought. She turned around to signal a nonverbal pre-apology to Seth for having to witness this mother-daughter debacle.

"No. I had sex with Jason."

"Jason?" That's right, Mom. Mr. Perfect.

"Jason."

Her mom twisted in her seat to look again at Seth. "Then why is Seth here?" she asked, still looking at him.

"Because he's my boyfriend. A really good one. *The* one."

Now Quinn turned around. She grinned at Seth. He grinned back.

Her mom shook her head. She signaled, pulling the car back onto the interstate. "I'll be damned," she muttered under her breath.

"I expected a bunch of protesters to swarm our car or something," her mom said twenty minutes later as she parked the Volvo in the Planned Parenthood lot. "It's so quiet."

"Maybe it's good that we're early," Quinn said. She'd scheduled the first appointment of the day, which still wasn't for a half hour. Now she sat twirling her hair so hard she'd probably end up with a single dreadlock. Her head throbbed. Her whole body had braced for scary drama. But the world didn't seem to notice or care that the three of them had just coasted into town for a Saturday morning abortion.

The outside of the clinic looked like any other boring doctor's office. It was a one-story brick building flanked by soft evergreens. It didn't look at all like a place where people acted on their personal crises. Tall clumps of wildflowers bloomed by the clinic's front door.

"Seth, you can stay in the car if you want," her mom said. "It's totally up to you. You're a champ for even showing up."

Quinn wondered if her mom wanted her daughter to herself. Seth seemed to be wondering the same thing. Quinn looked back and shrugged at him as if to say, "I'm not sure what the hidden message is."

"Sure," Seth said. "I'll read my magazine." He gestured to his *Harper's Magazine*. He stretched his arms across his seat. He looked exhausted.

Her mom smiled at his T-shirt du jour:

Aunt Em,

Hate you. Hate Kansas. Taking the dog.

- Dorothy

A Chevy Impala pulled in next to them. After shifting it into park, a girl Quinn's age with a short afro stared into her lap. She banged the steering wheel softly with both palms. When she felt the three of them staring at her, though, her face froze into a scowl. She sprung out of the car and slammed the door shut. Quinn and her mom exchanged a glance. They opened their doors. Seth got out of the car, too, to give Quinn a hug.

"I think we might be done with the sneaking around thing," he whispered in her ear.

"Yeah," she whispered back. "Totally busted."

She and her mom followed the other girl toward the clinic door.

With zero warning, the tall shrubs by the entrance spewed out a teenage guy with a crew cut, four pale middle-aged women, and an elderly man. The old man wielded a laminated poster of a bloody, dismembered fetus. The group of them blocked the way to the clinic entrance, circling Quinn, her mom, and the other girl, and shoved leaflets in their faces.

"Don't kill your baby! Please! We can help you!" Their eyes blazed as their voices screamed. The signs showed blood and tweezers and tiny limbs. One poster said, "One Dead, One Wounded."

Quinn's stomach lurched. Her knees wobbled. Her mom took her arm and fastened her eyes on the front entrance twenty feet away. Quinn desperately needed a bathroom.

The old man waved his bloody sign in her face, making her jump. Quinn got it. She really did understand that he wanted to protect human life. But why did he assume that a tiny embryo mattered more than Quinn's whole future? Why did these screeching Bible beaters think the answer to stopping abortion was to shame and scream at petrified teenage girls in parking lots? Why weren't they screaming at politicians for free birth control or something?

Getting pissed off made Quinn's knees wobble less. She drew herself up and took an enormous breath. She squeezed back on her mom's hand and kept walking. Ahead of them, though, the protesters were isolating the other girl in a weird, practiced formation. The girl tried to move forward.

"Don't let them murder your baby!" the old man begged her, six inches from the right side of her stony face. His age shocked Quinn—she wasn't in the habit of getting jostled and yelled at by old people. "You have other choices!" he screamed. "We can buy diapers! Please let us help you!"

The Chevy Impala girl spun around on her heel, startling the old guy and forcing him to take a step back. "You ain't got *nothing* to offer me! You understand what I'm saying?" she warned in a slow, shaky voice. With her left hand, she started ticking the fingers on her right. "I'm poor. I'm black. I'm flunking high school. My ma finds out about this and I got no place to live. You hearing me?" She got right in the old guy's face, forcing him to step back. "You ain't got nothing to offer me!"

The protesters finally backed off as if they knew they'd lost that battle. The girl tugged down the hem of her hooded sweatshirt and glided into the clinic like an empress in faded jeans. The door closed behind her. Now the protesters turned on Quinn and her mom.

"Look straight ahead, honey, and ignore them," her mom said quietly. "They want you to engage. Don't give them the satisfaction."

The group surrounded them quickly, forcing them to step backward instead of forward. As the entrance stretched farther out of Quinn and her mom's reach, angry bile pulsed up the back of Quinn's throat. These people didn't know the first thing about her. That wouldn't stop them from judging her, though, if she became a teenage mother. Their screaming made her falter. But her mom gripped her upper arm, making her hold her ground now. Quinn tried to see if Seth heard the commotion, but the blown-up photo of a dismembered fetus blocked her view.

"We can help you!" one of the older women shrieked again. Quinn wanted to haul off and smack her, threaten her. She wanted these fanatics to feel her own fear in its exact proportions. Her mom cleared her throat.

"Gee, honey, these people don't act like they want to help us. They act like they want to rip off our heads."

Quinn jumped at the sound of her mom's voice. Then she giggled in an unhinged sort of way. Her tears rose against her will. To get to the door now, they'd have to physically push through the screaming circle.

Out of the blue, Seth appeared on Quinn's other side. He squeezed his arm around her shoulders, holding her mom's relieved gaze for a grim second before facing straight ahead toward the entrance doors. Quinn took a shuddering breath to get some oxygen to her strangulated bloodstream. They could do this. With Seth's help now, they started pushing ahead. Quinn's terrified tears pooled again and spilled over, but now the entrance waited only six feet ahead, five.

"You'll go to hell for this!" the rabid-looking teenager shouted in her face while walking backward in front of her. Dots of white spit gathered in the corners of his mouth. Quinn stiffened inside the support sandwich that Seth and her mom had formed. Fierce and calm, Seth surged forward until he stood less than a foot away from the guy. He suddenly seemed taller than his five foot ten inches.

"Anti-choice men can go fuck themselves," Seth said. He pulled the door open and held it for Quinn and her mom, letting it close behind them with a faint whoosh.

They paused inside the foyer, doing a silent check-in with each other.

"Christ almighty," Quinn's mom said. That seemed to about cover it.

A man in a neon vest approached them, apologizing. He was a clinic escort, he said, a volunteer who helped patients get past the protestors. He'd taken a bathroom break before the start of his shift. Quinn's mom said something gracious to him before gesturing to Seth. "It's fine," she said. "We brought our own escort."

A half hour later, Quinn was sitting in an office the size of a broom closet. The woman she was with—Wanda—called herself an abortion counselor. Did she put that title on her business cards? Wanda's crispy, permed hair and big bangs washed out her complexion; she looked like a tired loaf of bread. Wanda shook Quinn's hand as she squeezed into a chair. She reached around for a plastic uterus sitting on the bookshelf.

The weird thing about the clinic—besides the rainbow of condoms in a bowl on the front desk—was its boringness. Quinn had expected something scarier or sleazier. Take away the nervous women and girls in the waiting room, and it was just another medical office. Someone had sponge-painted the walls a delicate lavender. Light-green chairs and cream-colored woodwork added to the vibe of cheerful calm.

Quinn checked out the safe sex posters on Wanda's wall and the plastic pelvis on the round Formica table between them.

"I studied all this in health class," she told Wanda.

"That's fine, Quinn. I'm just here to get your medical history and to make sure you have all the information you need. Okay?"

"Okay." As Quinn watched her own foot tap, Wanda took her blood pressure and asked about her past sexual partners, her last period, and the method of birth control she wanted. "One. Mid-March. None," she said.

"We'll need to send you home with birth control. You want the Pill? Condoms?" Wanda smiled. "We don't want to see you here again."

Quinn flushed. "We were using something. The condom broke," she explained. "I'm not like those girls in the waiting room."

Wanda's smile vanished. She sat up straight and pursed her lips.

"None of those girls are 'like those girls in the waiting room,' Quinn. No one dreams of growing up and one day having an abortion."

"Sorry." Quinn attempted a laugh. "What I meant was that after today, I can't imagine ever wanting to have sex again."

"I understand. But let's proceed on the assumption that in the distant future you might, okay? I'm sorry about the lecture, but everyone thinks they're a special case. I once had a Catholic schoolgirl in uniform tell me I was going to hell."

"But won't she burn in hell or whatever for being here herself?" Quinn's fists loosened in her lap.

"That's no one's business but hers."

Quinn nodded as she picked at a scratch in the table in front of her. "Do you think I'm doing the right thing?"

"That's not my call," said Wanda. "Anyone sitting in here with me probably has a reason. What is my business, though," she said, "is whether you've made this decision freely and with reliable information. Okay?"

"Okay."

"Should I put you down for the Pill?"

"Sure."

Wanda checked a box. "Who have you talked to about having an abortion?"

"My friend Ilene, my boyfriend, and my mom. She drove us."

"That's great."

"Do most girls tell their parents?"

"Most do," Wanda nodded. "Although for some, it's not safe."

"Not safe?"

Wanda ticked off the possibilities on her fingers. "Physically abused or neglected, emotionally abused or neglected, homeless . . ."

"Oh. Wow."

"Is anyone pressuring you to have an abortion?"

"No one besides me."

Wanda smiled briefly as she scanned her intake form. "You said your boyfriend knows?"

"Yes."

"And he's supportive?"

"Yes."

Wanda noted this in the file. "Sounds like you're a lucky girl."

Quinn smiled. *Lucky* wasn't how she would have described herself today but—considering things from Wanda's position—she guessed she was.

She hardly breathed as Wanda demonstrated an abortion on the fake pelvis, using blunt metal wands and plastic tubes. Quinn got queasy at "dilators." "Curettage instruments" and "suction" were definitely too much information. According to Wanda, the suction machine drew out "the contents of the uterus." That was the dumbest euphemism Quinn had ever heard. Why not call a spade a spade and an embryo and an embryo?

"Is anyone going to keep you company in the procedure room?" Wanda asked her.

Quinn shook her head. "My mom's a fainter. She says she'll be there in spirit."

Wanda smiled. "That's settled then. No fainters allowed." Quinn tasted the orange juice she'd had for breakfast.

It took four minutes. It hurt, but no worse than her monthly cramps. The friendly nurse told Quinn to breathe with her. She did, and it helped. The worst part was the horrible slurping sound, like a straw on the bottom of a milk shake. Then it was over. The doctor, a beefy guy with a gray beard, patted her trembling knee as he rose from his rolling stool. "You take care," he said.

"You, too," Quinn whispered.

The nurse put her in a wheelchair and pushed it down the hall into a quiet, sunlit room furnished with five La-Z-Boy recliners and side tables with cup holders. She settled Quinn into a chair. She covered her with a warmed blanket and peeled the tab off a can of apple juice.

"You can stay here as long as you like," the nurse said. "Most women stay an hour or more."

Women. Two days ago, that would have sounded like the wrong word. Now it fit.

"Thank you," Quinn said.

Her relief approached delirium. She wanted to kiss the nurse's hand or something. She looked around. Chevy Impala girl—reading a *People* magazine in the chair next to her—caught her eye. She raised her can of juice in a grim survivor's toast.

Quinn smiled. "We did it."

"We sure did."

CHAPTER 19
SELF-DEFENSE

Seth twitched as he sat near Quinn's mom in the waiting room. He'd taken his first morning off work in over a year so that he could sit here, surrounded by the evidence of the sex everyone else was having. That Quinn was not a virgin had become crystal clear at the movie theater. That made one of them.

Now he avoided Mrs. Ganey's eyes, pretending to read his magazine. He silently thanked God he hadn't been born a girl.

When he'd heard the protesters' shouts, his brain stopped. He didn't even realize that he'd sprung from the car until a minute later when he stood with Quinn and her mom in the lobby. All he knew at the time was that he wasn't going to let some crew-cut-sporting asshole mess with his girlfriend. Once they were inside, Quinn kept staring at him like she'd never seen him before—in a good way. That part he liked. He'd squeezed her hand when the overweight woman in a white clinician's coat called her name.

Crew Cut's shouting felt so personal, as though the guy saw Seth as the enemy or something. It was like Mr. Levine's perpetual question: is it simply easier to fight an enemy than it is to put your own house in order? Seth tried to put himself in the shoes of the protesters. They were afraid of something. Was it God's wrath or did they just get their undies in a bunch that women no longer had to stay barefoot and pregnant? Either way, their whole strategy was to make women the enemy. Seth's mom said that true Christianity was the practice of radical kindness. Maybe Crew Cut had missed church that day.

Seth looked around the clinic. This was not a place in which a red-blooded male expected to spend a Saturday. Especially for some other guy's screw-up. He repressed a smile. You can't make this shit up, he thought. He could write scripts for *Knots Landing* or something.

Quinn came back two hours later. The weak smile on her pale face told him and her mom that it was over.

None of them had had much breakfast. They ordered lunch at a Wendy's drive-through, each downing their Frostys before they even reached Omaha's city limits.

Seth sat in front with Mrs. Ganey—now in almost comfortable silence—as she drove straight into the early afternoon sun. Quinn slept across the backseat with his faded gray button-down shirt draped over her. Her cheek rested on her two palms pressed together like a little girl saying her prayers.

A center-pivot irrigation system blasted water into the air as they sped out of the Platte River valley. The landscape flattened again as riverbank pines gave way to grain fields and white farm buildings. From an airplane, Nebraska looked like a green-and-yellow checkerboard. Close up, Seth watched the breeze eddy across the fields like a kid had blown on a sink full of soap suds.

He stretched his legs, putting his right arm behind his head.

He imagined the cowboys, Indians, and buffalo that roamed these plains in past centuries. They must have felt powerful and immortal under a sky like this. Seth had never ridden a horse, but this would be the place to do it. You could go to the edge of the world if you wanted to, the pale blue dome above keeping you company.

"There's something honest about having it all out in plain view," he murmured to Mrs. Ganey. She dragged her eyes toward him—like her thoughts were a universe away. "Never mind." He shook his head and smiled. She smiled back, slipping away again into her thoughts.

Seth started to unwind. For once—at this exact moment—the fact of his own insignificance seemed reassuring instead of terrifying. He'd survived an actual gauntlet. He'd protected Quinn and won her mom's trust. He could feel himself dissolving into a version of himself that was still familiar, but also bigger and kinder than it used to be.

After school the next Friday, Seth ran home for a few minutes to help his mom.

"Why are you in such a good mood lately?" she asked as he placed her feet on the wheelchair footrests.

"Are you sitting down?" he asked. Teasing equaled love in their family.

"Ha-ha."

"I have a girlfriend."

She measured him with her good eye. "No!" she said, trying to slap the armrest. "Did hell freeze over?"

"Yes, it's true." He grinned at her. "Someone out there actually finds me attractive." He wheeled her up to the bathroom doorframe. As he gripped her waist and helped her rise to standing, his mom patted one of his hands.

"Of course she does. You're my beautiful boy," she said in a soft voice, serious now. "Is she wonderful? She'd better be."

"Yep," he said, holding her hands now as she shuffled forward. "She is wonderful. I'm headed to her house this afternoon if that's okay."

"Mind if I pee first?" Her wiseass side was back.

"Not as long as you hurry up. Tick tock."

He walked the mile and a half to Quinn's house. Now that he'd opened his big mouth, his mom wanted him to invite Quinn for dinner. That was so not going to happen yet. For starters, he didn't trust his mom to be on decent behavior. She could be a real bitch when she wasn't feeling well, although she didn't allow him to say *bitch*. Having never before brought home a girl, he also didn't trust himself not to act like a fool. He didn't totally trust Quinn either. It would suck if she met his mom and put on some kind of cheerful-around-handicapped-people bravado. More than one of his mom's new Lincoln friends had dumped her once they noticed that she was a real person with flaws, moods, and opinions—not their perky mascot.

Quinn held open her front door for Seth. Her house smelled like lemons and candles. It made him wonder what his own house smelled like. A collection of old photographs in black and silver frames filled the wall by the winding staircase. The Ganeys' house looked like it was waiting for the next party. In the living room, there were padded leather armchairs, a mission-style couch, and a worn oriental rug gathered around the fireplace. A bowl of tulips and a glossy art book sat on a polished coffee table. A Trivial Pursuit game in progress told Seth all he wanted to know about their wholesome family togetherness. He felt like a crusty-nosed kid pressing his face against a department store window.

Quinn was watching him. Seth adjusted his face to look like someone used to hanging out in fancy houses. He followed her into the dining room. A huge cat was belly flopped over a heap of tablecloth that had been shoved to one side of the table.

"Meet Elvis," Quinn said. Elvis was centered in a rhombus of late-afternoon sun. His foot rested on the base of a jam jar full of barely budding daffodils. He drooled on a stack of bills. Letters, stamps, and dishes cluttered the rest of the table along with a baby-blue Smith Corona typewriter. Okay, maybe the whole house didn't look like a movie set.

"Hi, Elvis." Seth scratched behind the cat's ears.

Quinn gestured to the table. "My mom's second office. She clears it off for dinner parties, then lets it decay back into its natural state." She waved Seth toward a heavy swinging door leading to the back of the house.

A graying, handsome guy sat at a small table in a sunny room next to the kitchen. He crunched on Wheat Thins while reading the *Wall Street Journal*.

"Hi, Dad," Quinn said casually.

Mr. Ganey looked guilty, like maybe he'd eaten a lot of Wheat Thins already. He smiled at Seth as Quinn introduced them. She sounded like she'd done this before, but also like someone who maybe was nervous.

Seth's mom had once told him to "dress for the job you want, not the one you have." As Quinn's father peered over his reading glasses at Seth's "That's All, Folks!" T-shirt, Seth wished he'd dressed for the girlfriend he wanted.

"It's nice to meet you, Mr. Ganey."

Quinn's eyes darted from him to her father and back to Seth again.

"Coke?" she asked. Seth nodded. She disappeared. Damn. If he'd known she'd have to leave the room to get it, he would have stayed thirsty.

"You're a senior, Seth?" Mr. Ganey asked, folding the newspaper.

"Yes, sir." So far, so good.

"Will you go to the U?"

Here we go. "I'll have to pay for college by myself, so I'm taking a year or two off to work." That could be true. He'd just never said out loud that he definitely planned to go to college.

Quinn returned with two red cans. She handed him one.

"I'll only be a minute, okay?" she asked.

Her eyes promised Seth that she wasn't throwing him to the dogs. He nodded.

"Let's move to the living room," her dad said to him. Seth would rather take some standardized tests. In a foreign language. He followed. "Do you live in the neighborhood?" Mr. Ganey asked, settling like the king of his castle in a leather armchair. He gestured for Seth to sit. Seth did.

"My mom and I live by Lincoln High." Four of his house would fit into this one. Mr. Ganey saw him check out the cover of a library book lying facedown by the chair. He held it up.

"Have you read this?" Mr. Ganey asked.

"No." *The Satanic Verses* had caused an international outcry, but no one Seth knew had actually read it. He was vaguely impressed. "How is it?"

"I've barely started it. I'm not a big fan of magical realism but wanted to see what all the fuss was about." He flashed a devious grin. Seth surprised himself by smiling back. "What about your dad?" Mr. Ganey asked. "Does he like to read?"

Seth jiggled his foot on his knee. "He died in Vietnam."

Mr. Ganey grimaced. "Gosh, I'm sorry to hear it," he said. "That's a rough deal." Seth didn't quite know how to handle sympathy from a wealthy Republican. Mr. Ganey leaned forward with his elbows on his knees and laced together his fingers. "The Vietnam War sure messed up a lot of things."

"Yeah, you won't catch me joining the army anytime soon."

"I can see why you'd feel that way," Mr. Ganey said, sitting back in his chair again. "Your family has sacrificed enough." Seth stopped jiggling his foot.

"Thank you." Oh, screw it. "No disrespect, sir, but the military has made all families sacrifice enough."

Mr. Ganey leaned his head back slightly, sizing up Seth. "The military didn't cause Vietnam," he said slowly. "A Democratic president started that war. The military carries out our policies. It's not a policy in and of itself."

"I'm not sure that's how Reagan saw things." Did Seth actually say that in his outside voice?

Mr. Ganey's eyes sparkled. He rubbed his hands together in slow motion and inspected his short, clean fingernails. "Not a fan, hey?" Seth shook his head with a small smile in spite of himself. "Reagan kept his eye on the ball, Seth. He built up America's defenses while making friends with Gorbachev. He set out to end the Cold War. It looks like he may have even pulled it off. That's no small accomplishment." He seemed pleased with himself, as if he'd ended the Cold War. Seth gripped the edge of the sofa cushion under his knees.

"Quinn mentioned you leaned to the right, Mr. Ganey."

"Call me Tom. Yeah," he said, "I'm old school. I want the government out of my pocket and out of my personal business. What about you?"

Seth considered his options but decided he was damned if he was going to tone down his opinions to win over this guy. "Reagan tripled our national debt. That's not anybody's idea of fiscally conservative."

"But that's all defense spending. Reagan's Strategic Defense Initiative—Star Wars, as the media likes to call it—was an investment in our national security. Reagan harnessed the free market and used its powers for good."

Seth rolled his eyes on the inside. Republicans talked about Star Wars like it solved everything. "You could also see Star Wars as a fake way to grow the economy and give contracts to your friends in the defense industry."

Mr. Ganey laughed, thank God. "I guess you're a Democrat?"

"Right." Gee, it showed?

"Reagan made Americans feel like themselves again. Yes, he spent more money than both of us would have liked. But consider the men before him. Carter brought us inflation and the hostage crisis after Johnson and Nixon brought us—all of us," he said, looking Seth in the eye, "heartache and cynicism. Reagan made us like ourselves again. There's nothing wrong with that."

"The Wizard of Oz made everyone like themselves, too," Seth said, grinning. There was something about this guy he liked, not his politics, obviously, but his surprising, honest interest in Seth's opinions.

Mr. Ganey looked startled for a second. Shit. Seth had gone too far. Then he guffawed. "Fair enough," Mr. Ganey said, shaking his head and smiling.

"Hi, Seth." Quinn stood blushing in the doorway. She'd put on her green sundress just for him.

Seth stood up. "You look great," he told her. Before he could catch himself, he glanced at Mr. Ganey, checking that it was okay to compliment a girl in front of her father.

Her dad smiled at him. "You do look nice," he told Quinn. To Seth he only half pretended to growl, "Have her home by eleven." When he held out his hand, Seth shook it.

"Did my dad interrogate you?" Quinn asked. They were sitting in a booth at Arturo's, a tiny Mexican restaurant downtown. She twirled with her finger the melted cheese stretching between her burrito and the bite on her fork.

"Yep." Seth folded a "tacha" before putting half of it in his mouth. The open-faced taco was broiled to greasy perfection. He had two orders of them sitting there on standby.

"Did I mention my dad is kind of intense?" She leaned over to sip from the straw in her Sprite. The glow from the candle in its red glass holder made that gesture look especially hot.

Seth fought his rising hard-on. This was not the time.

"I think you tried, but I wasn't paying attention. He's interesting."

"Right. Like how boa constrictors are interesting." A faint layer of lipstick stuck to the straw.

"Nobody's perfect." Seth didn't blame her for wanting to please her dad. Mr. Ganey had the privileged white guy thing going on for sure. But he also had a way of making you feel worthy. "He did tell me to call him Tom."

Quinn stopped eating midbite. Seth found himself staring at her wet tongue.

"Omigod, seriously? He's never . . ." She cut herself off.

"Never said that to any of your dozens of boyfriends?"

"Not dozens." He watched the familiar flush rise from her chest onto her neck and face.

"Maybe it's because none of those guys were as classy and good-looking as I am." He should change the subject before this one veered toward his relative inexperience. But Quinn changed it for him.

"That's definitely true," Quinn said. "My sister, Sarah, thinks you're God's gift, having never even met you."

"How so?"

"She wants me to tell you thanks," Quinn said in a low, quiet voice.

Seth ducked his head. "Tell her I said, you're welcome."

"I will."

"About that last boyfriend . . ." Seth said. Quinn shook her head violently. "Okay, about your current boyfriend . . ."

"What about him?"

"He wants to get you alone."

"Did you know O Street is the longest street in America?" Quinn asked him five minutes later as she turned her mom's car onto Twenty-Seventh Street.

"Really?" He squeezed her thigh. "I thought it only felt that way."

She smiled, pulling onto a side street bordering the Sunken Gardens and parking the car.

He swung her hand as they circumnavigated on foot the acre-sized bowl of landscaping. She admired the iris and columbine on its graveled walking paths. The humidity made the seventy-degree May weather feel even hotter, although clouds were gathering and wind blew in small puffs. A few minutes later, Seth used a ten-second sprinkle of rain as an excuse to pull her toward privacy: a vine-covered wall sheltered by a tree with pink buds ready to burst.

He pressed her against the gray stone. Strands of her fine hair fanned against the ivy. She welcomed his soft kisses. And when he stroked her breasts through the fabric of her bra, she scrunched his shirt in fistfuls around his ribs. She let him slide a foot between hers. When he pressed their thighs together, she sighed and pressed back. But when he rubbed his boner against her, she pulled away.

"I'm so not ready for that."

Got it. Message received. He backed off and ran a hand over his face and through his hair. He scuffed at some woodchips with his shoe. "Are you mad at me?" he asked her.

"No, of course not."

"Are you mad at you?"

"No. Yes. Maybe." Seth hoped Quinn wasn't planning to take a chastity vow or something for the duration. He was trying really hard not to act like a pervert, but his horniness bordered on something like frantic. "Sorry," she said. "I'm in a weird mood. Maybe I'll just take you home."

"I'll walk," he said. "It's only six blocks."

"I didn't mean to offend you."

"You didn't. Neither of us can help it if I think you're hot."

Quinn smiled. She looked relieved. "Remind me again why you're with me? Besides wanting to get in my pants?"

"Because you're such a goddamn mess, obviously. I thought being with someone sunny and stable like I am would do you some good."

Now she laughed. "No, really," she said quietly. Seth tucked her hair behind her ear.

"Because you're the kindest person I've ever met. Because you're smart. Because I like myself best when I'm with you." He kissed her lightly and waved her toward her car.

He went home and jerked off. *Playboy* wasn't the real thing, he thought as he lay on his bed, panting. But it sure took the edge off.

CHAPTER 20
CLASS STRUGGLE

Quinn called Trish the next morning. The guilt was eating her alive. She didn't admit that she and Seth had been sneaking around for weeks, only that they'd gone out a few times.

"What is it you like about him?" Trish asked, yawning.

"He's smart," Quinn said. "Funny, too, when you get to know him." From her perch on the washing machine, she could see into the neighbors' yard. Sharp fans of yellow iris burst out of some rake-lined dirt. Crumbs of detergent had spilled across the surface of the dryer. Quinn pushed them into a small heap. She then divided it into pie slices with her fingernail as she breathed in the smell of bleach.

"Maybe he's changed in the last five years," Trish conceded. "We're not exactly buddies, though, so leave me out of any double dates, okay?"

"Last I checked, you weren't dating anyone."

"True, although it's obnoxious of you to mention it. Drew and I are going to prom, though. As friends." Quinn made a face. Trish apparently heard it through the phone. "I know. But he can dance."

"Trish, there's one more thing." Silence. "I had an abortion. A week ago. I didn't tell Jason, but I told my mom, and she was cool. She took me to Omaha." Quinn wasn't ready to tell Trish about Seth's role—it would make her jealous. "Trish? Are you mad I didn't tell you sooner?"

Trish let out a lungful of air. "No."

"That's all you have to say?" This didn't feel very supportive.

Trish sniffled. "I had an abortion, too. Last summer. Quinn, I wanted to tell you. I really did. But I felt too stupid, like, 'Quinn would never get herself into such a mess.'"

"Ha," Quinn said. "You give me way too much credit."

"I guess so." Trish laughed.

"Plus, we didn't get ourselves into a mess all by ourselves. And we're not stupid. We're human. No better and no worse than anyone else."

"That's true. And you feel okay now? No problems?"

"No problems. I napped for a day. That was it," Quinn said. "What about you?"

"Same," said Trish. "Just like you said: no better and no worse than anyone else."

As Quinn and Seth approached his house a few days later, she pretended not to see that the window boxes still held last year's dead flowers and parched vermiculite. It looked like a potted plant graveyard. Quinn tripped on a corner of the cement walk and squeezed Seth's arm to regain her balance.

"Easy there," Seth joked. "You haven't even met her yet." His low, sexy laugh made her wonder for the hundredth time why she had wasted most of high school dating guys who weren't Seth. All she wanted was to be alone with him.

The hollow-core front door echoed Seth's brief knock before he unlocked it and held it open for her. Quinn knew how to be a parent pleaser, but her stomach tightened like a fist. Seth had been annoyingly vague about what his mom was like. The small entryway squeezed them out into a cramped living room that smelled like kitty litter and dryer sheets.

A freckled woman with a slight, boyish body and a clawed right hand squinted up at them from a wheelchair that sat next to the couch facing the door. A calico cat leaped off her lap, knocking a new library book onto the floor. "There goes my desk," she said with a wry smile, Seth's smile. "Come in." She gestured with the thick-handled magnifying glass she grasped in her left hand.

Cat hairs covered Seth's mom's loose shirt and sweatpants. They sprouted from the Velcro tabs on her gym shoes. As Seth and Quinn drew closer, Mrs. Burton looked her over. Seth introduced them.

"It's nice to meet you, Mrs. Burton," she said. One of her mom's friends—a paraplegic—had told Quinn once that it was rude for the "temporarily abled" to tower over people in wheelchairs. A surge of careless adrenaline made Quinn seat herself in the corner of the couch next to her. Seth's mom's intent eyes showed the briefest flicker of surprise.

"Call me Debbie," she said. Her left shoulder rode higher than her right. The strands escaping her loose ponytail softened her sharp pixie face, but the smile she aimed in Quinn's direction didn't quite reach her penetrating eyes.

Between them, a small table held what Quinn realized was the debris of an entire existence. It included magazines, a bottle of pills, a felt-tipped pen wrapped in a thick layer of bike handle tape, Kleenex, and a cereal bowl half-full of unwrapped Tootsie Rolls and cinnamon discs. Quinn chewed the inside of her cheek, trying to think of something nonstupid to say.

"So you're the famous Quinn," Debbie said, scrutinizing her sideways. Seth had mentioned that the MS made his mom favor her left eye. Her squint made her look skeptical.

"Mom, for God's sake," Seth said. "Ease up." Debbie laughed. He seemed embarrassed, but Quinn saw his body relax a little like they'd all cleared some invisible hurdle.

"Geez, can't a girl ask a few questions?" Debbie said.

"Nope," Seth replied. They must have exchanged some kind of signal, because he got up and walked over to her. "Be right back," he told Quinn. He wheeled his mom toward the bathroom.

Quinn looked around the living room. It wore a style she recognized from Trish's apartment-living days as rental-property tired: dirty cream walls huddled around stained beige shag carpeting. She could hear Trish's disdain in her head, like Scarlett O'Hara in a mint-green Limited sweater and matching Mia flats, swearing she'd never go hungry again. If you grew up poor, how long did it take you to let down your guard once you reached safe ground?

The spare furniture made a path for Debbie's wheelchair. On top of a small television, a water glass decaled with a faded Ronald McDonald held a bunch of magenta lilacs. Quinn liked the loud mix of orchids, African violets, and pots of forced daffodils on wicker tables that took up the full width of the room's west-facing double windows. A ripped plastic tablecloth spread underneath and extended out into half the room. A brown plaid recliner with threadbare arms held a basket of unfolded, clean laundry. There were framed prints of modernist paintings on the walls that Quinn knew: Picasso's *Three Musicians*, a Georgia O'Keeffe flower, a National Gallery print of a Mark Rothko square.

The wallpaper peeled near the ceiling in the dining room. The bars of late-afternoon sunlight slanting through the plastic shades did the pattern way more harm than good.

She heard the toilet flush. When Seth and his mom came back, Quinn stood to make room for Debbie to park her chair. Seth moved a sleeping orange cat so that he could sit next to Quinn on the couch. He must have redone his mom's ponytail.

"Who's that?" Quinn asked, pointing to the orange cat.

"Sid Not-So-Vicious," Debbie said.

"And that?" Quinn asked, pointing to the calico in the window.

"Nancy. So, Quinn. Seth tells me you're going to . . ." Debbie held up her hand to keep Seth from reminding her. "George Washington?"

"Yes."

"It's a hard time to meet someone new." It sounded like an accusation, like the irony of getting together right before graduation hadn't occurred to them. It was too early in her and Seth's relationship to make plans and too late not to care. Seth collapsed against the back of the couch and smacked his forehead.

"Mom, c'mon!" he groaned. "It's been all of one month! Can we pick this apart another time? Like never?"

Debbie leaned back in her wheelchair. As Sid crept over and circled in her lap, she smiled at Seth. This time it reached her eyes. Their kitchen seemed to vibrate with yellowness. Only the orange-flecked countertops and pocked linoleum floor had apparently escaped an enthusiastic painting project. Quinn reached toward the knotted cord on the wall phone. It needed to dangle for a minute and unwind. She stopped herself midreach, though, and hoped that Seth hadn't noticed her acting like a dork.

He leaned into the refrigerator. When he stood tall again, he jerked his head toward the living room, rolled his eyes, and blew out an exaggerated breath. He tossed her two apples, one at a time. After he had found her a paring knife, she positioned the apples upright. She looked over at him for direction and noticed the soft tan skin under his collarbones. He caught her staring. He put an arm around her waist and pulled her toward him. He planted a kiss on her like they were in a 1940s movie. She loved the way he kissed: sweet and shy at first and then . . . not. He let her go and grinned. She blushed. Must. Get. A grip.

"Cubes or slices?"

"Doesn't matter."

"I mean, are we baking them or eating them raw?"

"Eating them. With spaghetti."

Quinn sliced the apples and fanned them on a thin, white plate. Seth turned a dial on the stove. When the gas clicked, he lit three burners with a match that he then tossed into the sink without even looking. He dumped a jar of Food 4 Less pasta sauce into one pan and heated another full of water. Pulling a can out of a cupboard, he asked her with his eyes if she liked beets. She nodded. In her opinion, beets tasted like pearls of dirt, but she kept this to herself.

She offered to make garlic toast. He found her some bread and margarine in the fridge and excavated garlic from a small, sticky collection of spice jars. He broke the spaghetti into the pot while Quinn shaved off curls of hard margarine with her paring knife. She squished them onto the soft bread.

"If I'd known you were going to make me cook," she said, "I would have picked a different guy." He smiled into the pasta pot. Then he threw a heel of bread at her. He kissed her again as he helped her pick the crumbs out of her hair. Quinn set the dining room table as he helped his mom. At her own house, they'd have tossed salad and steamed fresh vegetables with their pasta. Her mom would set the table with placemats and candles. Seth waited for Debbie to mark the page in her book.

"Ready?" he asked her.

"Ready," she said.

He scooted behind her and pushed her chair toward the dining room.

"Can I help, or should I just stay out of the way?" Quinn asked. A little red wagon stood in the corner of the dining room, holding cleaning supplies, like a cheerful art installation scoffing at her awkwardness.

"Just stay out of the way," Debbie warned cheerfully.

As Seth rolled her up to the table, Quinn saw Debbie notice the garlic bread. Seth cut up his mom's spaghetti with the side of his fork before sitting up straight in his chair and twirling his own pasta into a spoon.

"Quinn," Debbie asked, "have you decided what to study next year?"

"Not really. But I tell people that I'm prelaw."

"Are you prelaw?"

Quinn smiled. "I have no idea."

Seth laughed.

"Seth is going to college, too, someday," Debbie said. Seth's pasta twirling slowed.

"He told me," Quinn said. "I bet he could get in anywhere."

Debbie gave her a sharp look. "When the timing's right, he'll go to the university here. Unfortunately, I'm kind of high maintenance right now." Her brittle laugh made Seth flinch. "I'd hate for him to start the semester and then have to drop out."

Seth had said this, but Quinn suddenly noticed the subtle, affectionate outlines of the trap in which he lived. "When do you think he should apply?" Quinn asked, studying her apple slices. She glanced at Seth. His face warned her.

"That depends on my health. What they don't tell you in those stupid feel-good movies is that being disabled sucks. And it sucks for everyone involved."

Quinn flinched, knowing she should stop talking. Multiple sclerosis only got worse. But if MS called the shots, Seth might not start college for years.

Debbie scrutinized her from the end of the table like a spider sizing up its next meal.

Sitting here in this kitty-litter-smelling house with an overprotective single mom in a wheelchair suddenly irritated her, like Quinn should feel guilty for existing or something. It wasn't her fault that Debbie and Seth had shitty luck. And why was Debbie so negative? Didn't she want a better life for her son?

"Maybe next year," Quinn said, backing down.

"By then Seth will be eighteen and my AFDC will have run out," Debbie said.

Quinn turned to Seth. "AFDC?" her eyes asked.

"Aid for Dependent Children." he told Quinn softly. He frowned at his plate and slumped down in his chair.

Quinn saw the familiar self-defeat he often wore at school. She couldn't think of anything—tactful or otherwise—to say about he and his mom being on welfare. "Oh," she conceded to Debbie with a small smile. "That sucks, too." Mostly for Seth. His mom was telling him to fly but wouldn't let him use his wings.

Seth pulled the front door closed behind them. They sat on the step. The people living across the street had evidently stored all their worldly possessions on their screened front porch. The dog staked in the yard next door trotted in weary circles as the sunshine faded. Fast clouds mellowed into hazy stillness as the sky thinned into grays and pinks. Quinn nudged Seth with her elbow.

"That was fun," she said.

Seth let out a snort. "Which part? Doing my chores or tangling with my mom?"

"You thought that was tangling? You met my dad, right?" She opened her mouth to say something else, but Seth squished her in a sideways hug. He smelled like sawdust and lotion. Quinn leaned her head into his neck. She turned and kissed it in the circular motions that he liked. He groaned and lifted his chin for more.

Her stomach did a slow, now-familiar flip. She'd spent years feeling like something was waiting for her just around the corner if only she could get to it. It had been leading up to this. But this wasn't a nameless craving: this felt like an addiction, a reckless, physical high of affection. It made her want to tap dance in front of the whole world.

"Seth? Let's go to prom."

"Prom?" he rasped. She could tell it had never crossed his mind, let alone while they were making out. But it would be fun to show up as a couple. Romantic.

"Think about it." Then she looked at her watch. She sighed. "I should go home."

It was a school night, and she still had homework. Seth stood and pulled her to her feet. He draped his arm over her shoulder as he walked her to the car. The dense planes of his arms and chest against her made her feel fluid and soft in comparison. He guided her to the driver's side and then blocked the door by leaning back against it. His brown eyes teased and invited her.

"Is your mom watching us?" Quinn asked.

"Nope."

He tugged her hair a little to bring her closer. She leaned against him, toes to toes, chest to chest. He pressed his lips to hers and lingered for a long, soft smooch. When he touched her tongue with his, the rushed sound of her own exhale took her by surprise.

CHAPTER 21
MUTUALLY ASSURED DESTRUCTION

The way Quinn kissed his neck made Seth forget who he was. One of the drawbacks of extreme sexual arousal, however, was that when she'd asked him again that night almost two weeks ago to go with her to prom, he hadn't had the presence of mind to say no.

Now, though, what he felt was active dread. Okay, maybe *dread* was too strong a word. Compared with, say, liking a girl for almost three years and working up the nerve to tell her, prom didn't qualify for *dread*. It was like when he asked his mom about her pain levels. "Compared to childbirth?" she'd say. "Zero." His mom's favorite motto was "Buck up or fuck off." She and her stoic Swedish ancestors could write cards for Hallmark.

"Quinn, you look beautiful," his mom said now as Quinn walked through their front door wearing a silky green dress. His mom only smiled with her mouth, though, an expression Seth recognized as a camouflage for pain.

In the past few weeks Seth had made two trips to the pharmacy. A month ago, his mom had still kept her pain medication doses low; she still wanted to claim sobriety. But now she didn't talk about sobriety. These days, actually, she talked less in general. Aunt Gail—after making his mom's bed—had recently threatened to toss the dingy pillowcases and splurge on new ones. Seth could tell from the smile on Gail's face that she expected to do the usual bossy battle with her sister. But Seth's mom had said something like, "Whatever you think, Gail. Thanks." Her head wasn't in it.

Quinn did look beautiful. Plus her strapless dress showed skin that he'd touched under her shirt, but never actually seen. She'd pinned up her hair in a twisty knot.

"Thank you," Quinn told his mom. "Seth cleans up good, too, don't you think?"

"He does indeed," his mom said. Now her smile flickered for a second into her eyes. Seth admitted to himself that maybe it had been worth it to use fifty bucks of his small college stash to rent a tux and uncomfortable shoes. He mentally downshifted from dread to wariness. He leaned over to hug his mom goodbye. Quinn did the same, surprising his mom, who gave her a trembling pat in return while locking eyes with Seth.

As they drove to East Campus, he felt himself relax. Thank God they'd skipped the fancy restaurant routine. Two hours earlier, they'd sat in a green booth at Runza drive-through and eaten burgers in their jeans and T-shirts. They'd joked about their classy preprom onion breath. All day the sky had had a looming-tornado vibe to it, glowing with a slightly menacing yellow vapor. It never did quite change, though, into the telltale creepy green of impending tornado violence.

They approached the student union ballroom from an echoing hallway. Ahead of them, Trish burst out of the bathroom. Seth had to admit that her peach-colored mermaidy dress made her ass look especially good. But when Quinn called, "Hello," Trish's smile faded into something more like a stomachache. Seth ventured a half-hearted wave.

"Hey," he said.

"Hey," said Trish.

Quinn raised her eyebrows at Trish as if to say, "Really? That's the best you can do?"

"Are you coming?" Quinn asked her out loud, gesturing down the hall toward the sound of dance music.

"You two go ahead," Trish said before clicking away in the other direction.

The strings of lights and paper decorations tried to copy *Pretty in Pink*. Christ. Seth's worst nightmare was more like it. He pushed out his chest as they walked into the dance, putting on what he hoped was a confident expression. He told himself to relax; it wouldn't kill him to suck it up for a couple of hours and pretend to have fun for Quinn's sake. It was remotely possible, too, that he actually would have fun.

Quinn waved to a group of her girlfriends across the room. A second later, she was letting go of his hand and squealing, "You look great!" while rushing over to their table. Seth stood alone, still barely inside the ballroom. He scanned the room for friendly faces. Terrence waved at him from the table Quinn was walking toward. Seth followed at a distance as she and her friends talked in that relentless language girls use with each other: fast, high, and always interrupting.

He caught up to her and pulled out her chair like a gentleman. Their table bordered the dance floor. Trish sat down next to Drew. Seth nodded a wary greeting. Drew slurred, "What's up," through a self-satisfied, douchebag smile. He was the kind of idiot who'd bore his kids senseless in twenty years with stories of his glory days playing varsity football. Seth wanted to crack up Quinn by whispering this in her ear, but she was facing the girl on her left and paying zero attention to him. She also gave off a weird, low-level hum of tension. This whole thing had been a bad idea.

Trish swayed slightly in her folding chair. She and Drew were drunk, Seth realized. Why hadn't he thought to drink a few beers earlier? He watched his classmates gyrate to a sixties song from the *Dirty Dancing* soundtrack.

Terrence watched him, smiling, before gesturing to Seth to take the seat next to him. Seth sat down. Terrence wore his trademark Nike Velcro high-tops with his rented formal wear. Now Seth wished he'd worn his Chuck Taylors to show that he didn't take this thing too seriously. These tight rented slip-on loafers felt like a metaphor for the whole stupid charade.

"Hey, man. Nice tux," Terrence said.

Even sober, Seth did feel kind of handsome in spite of his itchy collar. "Thanks," Seth said. "You, too. Who's your date?" he asked, looking around the table.

"Came solo." Under his breath he said, "My boyfriend told me he didn't feel like getting beat up tonight." Boyfriend? This was news. That Terrence had just come out to him was flattering. It also put his own minor drama into perspective.

"I think you should question the guy's commitment," Seth replied quietly. "Can it be true love if he's not willing to take a punch in the face?"

Terrence laughed softly. "Thanks, man. Who are you with?"

"Quinn asked me."

Terrence widened his eyes and nodded, impressed. "I've known her since kindergarten," he said. "She's all that. Aren't you, Quinn?" he shouted at her across Seth.

As Quinn turned to talk now to Terrence, she at least included Seth in her line of vision. But she kept glancing from him to her girlfriends when she thought he wasn't looking, like she didn't quite understand what he was doing there. That made two of them.

"I'm gonna bounce," Terrence told him a few minutes later.

Seth gripped Terrence's forearm for melodramatic effect. He murmured, "Take me with you." He gestured to the girls. "I don't understand their language."

Terrence laughed. "You could ask her to dance."

"Yeah, and monkeys might fly out of my butt."

Terrence laughed. "Party on, Wayne."

"Party on, Garth."

"Did you see *Saturday Night Live* last weekend?" Terrence asked. "Dana Carvey was doing President Bush. He had this whole 'breeze of democracy' thing about China. That guy kills me." Terrence squeezed Seth's arm as he stood up and left.

Now Seth and Drew were the only ones at the table not in a

conversation. Drew checked him out like a scientific curiosity in a glass jar.

"Dude," he sneered. "Mr. Levine, like, loves you. You're, like, his favorite student." Apparently Drew thought he sounded like some kind of streetwise LA skateboarder.

Quinn's eyes skittered back and forth between them as he and Drew locked eyes in visual combat.

"I heard this DJ at my cousin's wedding," Quinn announced to the table in a loud rush. Drew ignored her.

"I'm serious," he continued with a soft burp. "Does Levine slip you the answers before class or something? How do you know all that lefty propaganda?"

"I read. You should try it sometime," Seth said.

Quinn gripped his thigh under the table as a warning.

"Are you fucking with me?" Drew asked. "Do not go there, man."

"Look, *man*," Seth said. "I'm not going anywhere. All I'm doing is sitting here with my girlfriend, minding my own business."

Quinn stiffened when he said the word *girlfriend*. What the hell had happened to the ballsy girl who threw hamburgers at Drew's face? Quinn glared at both of them. Drew rolled his eyes at him before losing interest.

Seth would make one more effort. If it didn't work, he'd bail. He asked Quinn to dance. People stared as they walked onto the parquet dance floor. But he chilled out a little when the DJ spun a slow song; he could pull off a slow dance without looking like a total fool. He put his arms around Quinn's waist. He smiled at her, trying for a do-over.

The song turned out to be "Eternal Flame." The Bangles' lead singer's voice totally encapsulated prom: saccharine and generic, with delusions of its own grandeur.

"Man, I fucking *hate* this song," he groaned.

"Shocker," Quinn snapped as she pulled away from him. She looked around to see if anyone had overheard. Seth stared at her. "I mean, if the music isn't U2 or The Ramones or some deadly depressing fringe band, you pitch a tantrum." She opened her mouth as if to say more, then closed it. "You didn't have to come, you know."

"I wanted to," Seth said, his voice a warning. As his jaw tensed, his collar choked him.

Quinn pressed her lips into a straight line. "You know what? You walked in here assuming that every person in this room is a snob. But you're the biggest snob here."

Seth rammed his fists in his pockets. "What's your problem?"

"I don't have a problem." Quinn put her hands on her hips. "You do. You tell yourself how smart you are and judge everyone else. But what you're really doing is sitting on the sidelines." Seth's anger whipped right past his confusion. Who was the bitch in the green dress? "You'd rather whine about not going to college instead of admitting that you could make it happen if you wanted to."

"Fuck you, Quinn," he hissed. "What do you know about actual responsibility?" He heard the nasty edge in his voice but didn't care. Quinn's face turned red, but her eyes stayed narrowed and angry. "I'm sorry my blue-collar future isn't good enough for you, but I could have shouted that up to you in your ivory tower before you asked me out."

Quinn turned and walked toward the lobby, squeezing through the crowd of slow dancers. Seth hesitated, then followed. She turned around to face him when they reached the drafty entrance.

"This isn't about me! Your 'blue-collar future' isn't good enough for *you*! Why are you willing to fight for all those lost political causes but not for yourself? I mean, you're an amazing son to your mom, and it's great that you support her, but her disease is just shitty luck. Why have you just put your head down like it's your fault?"

Seth thought about his cousin Lee in his Sears jumpsuit. He'd be damned if he ended up like Lee, making minimum wage forever. But he'd also be damned if he were going to listen to one more word from a stuck-up brat whose parents had already paid her college bill. This girl's hardest choice so far had been taken care of with $250 and a drive to Omaha. And yet she was still talking.

"Who gets a thirty on the ACT and doesn't even apply to college?" she asked. "You're using your mom as an excuse. And you know what's even worse? She's letting you."

"Who the hell do you think you are?" Jabbing his chest, he shouted, "And who do you think I am? Your little third-world buddy that you get to swoop down and fix? You don't know fuck all about me and the reality I live in."

He flung open an exit door and stalked out. He'd been a fool to think a rich girl—even Quinn—could appreciate what it was to be poor and screwed. He just couldn't do this anymore.

CHAPTER 22
PROXY WARS

"**D**rew has vodka in the car," Trish slurred in Quinn's ear, slipping down slightly in her folding chair. Walking back to the table after Seth stormed out, Quinn had felt twenty pounds lighter. She'd agreed to cheeseburgers for dinner; but would it have killed him to let her have fun with her friends without wearing scorn all over his face?

"I have some smokes. Let's go," Quinn said.

Trish let out a whoop. They held hands and ran on tiptoe in their high heels as light rain sprinkled the warm asphalt parking lot. The green-yellow haze of an impending storm still hung in the near dark. They gathered their dresses and bounced into the back of Drew's VW Rabbit. Trish pulled out the clear bottle of booze from underneath the seat as Quinn pulled two cigarettes out of her beaded purse and stuck both in her mouth. She lit them with a black lighter. She passed one to Trish and took the offered bottle. The nasty taste hardly bothered her after a few swallows. Trish laughed.

"What would your boyfriend think of you now?"

"I couldn't care less," Quinn lied.

She leaned her head sideways against the window, then un-rolled it to blow out a deep drag of smoke. When Seth let down his guard—like he did when they were alone—he filled the room with silent calm and kindness. And he looked hot in a tux. Their plan had been to leave the dance early and make out in her dad's car. But from the minute they'd walked into the student union, his judgmental, above-it-all act came out. Quinn tapped her ash over the top of the window and felt the vodka buzz build.

"God, what was I thinking? I thought it would be romantic to suddenly show up as a couple. And then I totally choked. But then again, it's like he won't let me be on his side until I offer a blanket apology for being wealthy or something," she said. "I'm sick of it."

"C'mon, Quinn." Trish opened her own window. "Did you honestly think you and he would last? I bet he took one look at you in that dress and finally realized that he's not in your league."

Quinn shrugged. "He liked my fancy dress." She reached again for the vodka.

"I'm sure. He probably thought you got it at Kmart."

Quinn thunked the bottle back down onto the seat between her knees.

"Go to hell, Trish."

Trish's head jerked up as she flicked her cigarette out the window. "Excuse me?"

"Why are you so hard on him? Why do you act as though him going out with me is so bizarre? It's like you think it makes you look bad. Why is this about you?"

Trish closed her eyes and shook her head like a baby refusing a spoonful of squash. "I don't know what you're talking about."

"I think he reminds you of yourself." Quinn knew she was going too far, but the vodka wouldn't let her reel herself back in. "You act like him being poor and unlucky is contagious or something. But you of all people should know better."

Trish's eyes snapped. "That's stupid. I just don't want my best friend to be with a guy who can't appreciate her."

Quinn threw her cigarette out into the rain. The orange tobacco end got pummeled into brown mush. She felt her adrenaline start to fade, trailing the lonely aftertaste of bravery. "That's why I broke up with Jason! He's the guy who didn't appreciate me!" Tears streamed down her cheeks. "Trish," she whispered. "Don't you know me?"

Trish turned to stare at her. Then she reached for the door handle. "I guess not."

The soles of Trish's pumps ground against the parking lot grit as she pulled herself out of the car. She slammed the door behind her.

Quinn's dad answered after eight rings.

"Yes?" he demanded.

"Dad, it's me," Quinn blurted into the student union pay phone. She hurried to add, "I'm okay." He waited. "Seth and I broke up. He left. I've been drinking. Will you come get me?"

Her dad cleared his throat. "You're on East Campus?"

"Yeah."

"With my car?"

"Yeah."

"We'll be there in twenty minutes." He hung up.

Quinn leaned too hard against the brick wall. Fifteen minutes later, her dad climbed out of her mom's car and walked toward the building entrance where Quinn still stood. Her mom waited until Quinn and her dad climbed into his car. They followed her mom's taillights.

"Do you want to talk about it?" her father asked. He wore jeans and his pajama shirt. His hair stuck up around the crown of his head.

"Not especially." Quinn felt too out of it to talk to anyone, least of all her dad.

"Is Seth alright?"

"I guess."

"Does he need a ride, too?"

What, was he on Seth's side now? Quinn shook her head. Seth would already be home. She started to cry.

Her dad reached over the armrest and squeezed her knee. "You and Seth are very different people," he ventured. "That can be hard on a relationship."

Quinn's head throbbed. Her throat burned as if her stomach hadn't yet decided if it was going to throw up. "What do you know about it?" She didn't mean to be rude. She just wanted to be left alone.

Her dad swatted down the left-turn signal and cleared his throat as he adjusted the windshield wiper. "Let me give you this advice, Quinn." His voice sounded like cold branches snapping under the weight of wet snow. "Quit smoking my cigarettes. And stop talking."

They rode in silence until they pulled into the garage. Her mom got out of her car in the next bay and waited for them. Her dad turned off the engine and turned in his seat to look squarely at Quinn.

"I'm mad as hell," he said slowly. "And I'm glad you called us. Do you understand?"

"Yes," she whispered, avoiding his eyes.

CHAPTER 23
PEACEKEEPERS

Mr. Levine had written a quote on the chalkboard:

> "I believe that we are on an irreversible trend
> toward more freedom and democracy—but that
> could change."
> **-VICE PRESIDENT DAN QUAYLE**

What a moron. Seth hunched over his desk, ignoring Quinn when he wasn't sneaking glimpses at her. Her left hand scrunched half her face as she held her head with it. She doodled in her notebook with the other. She only half turned when Ilene spoke to her.

Seth had walked the several miles home from the university's East Campus. In the dark he'd yanked off his tie and pushed it into the pocket of his tux. The next day, he'd gotten a raise and a promotion at the lumberyard. He should have been happy, but it hit him like a taunt, a cosmic kick in the ass.

The breeze sliding under the windows could barely compete with the greenhouse effect of the baking afternoon sunlight angling through them. The room smelled like armpits and stale coffee. Mr. Levine faced the class. He had upside-down chalk handprints on the knees of his gray jeans.

"What do we know about the people who are overthrowing communist governments or trying to get rid of colonial rulers?"

"They're really, really pissed off," a girl said.

Seth knew something about being pissed off. He'd waited for Quinn to call these last two days and apologize. She hadn't. Over the weekend, he'd caught his mom watching him. When she'd asked him about prom, he'd been a total asshole and told her to mind her own business. Her eyes had flashed at him.

"Fine," she'd said. "But it's no picnic standing by while that little brat jerks you around!" Seth had walked away; he wasn't going to stand there and defend Quinn. He should have burned that stupid love note the minute he'd written it.

He scanned the room for a focal point that wasn't Quinn. He'd be the last guy to judge another man's housekeeping. But the dirty coffee cups teetering in a crooked stack on the edge of Mr. Levine's desk had been there for two weeks. The brown dribble down the front of the desk, though, was new.

"How can America help without making things worse?" Mr. Levine asked. "Seth?"

Seth knew something about arrogant, ignorant do-gooders who dabbled in other people's problems.

"The U.S. could shut up and listen, for starters," he lobbed in Quinn's direction. She jumped a little. When she met his gaze, it felt like she was standing on his chest.

"Ah," said Mr. Levine, looking back and forth between the two of them. "If we did that, what would we hear from people whose relatives were murdered and whose children were starving?"

"Maybe we'd hear that they don't necessarily want to be mini Americas," Seth said. "Maybe they're not short on plans and ideas. Maybe they only need some cash and food and a fair chance." He did want to go to college. He didn't care if that made him a sellout.

Trish glared at him. He returned the favor until she turned away.

A corner of Quinn's mouth turned up.

"Shouldn't we make them first promise to become capitalist democracies like the United States?" Mr. Levine asked.

Quinn turned in her seat to address Seth alone. "Not unless we want them to stay really, really pissed off," she said. Her smile apologized. Seth smiled back. Mr. Levine jingled the change in his pocket.

"Foreign aid can't fix everything, folks. For example, what do we do now as thousands of young Chinese march for democracy in Tiananmen Square? What if we help the students?"

"We piss off the Chinese government," said the girl behind Quinn.

"What if we support the government?"

"We look like hypocrites," Seth said. Quinn still watched him.

"What if we do nothing?"

"We seem friendly to fascists," said another guy.

"Right," said Mr. Levine. "And what happened the last time the world went soft on fascism?"

"Germany took over Europe," said Ilene.

"So what do we do?" Mr. Levine asked.

"Talk to both sides," said Quinn.

"I see. And use different levels of diplomacy?"

Quinn nodded.

"But isn't that what Reagan did in South Africa?" Seth interrupted. The class—including Quinn—turned to look at him.

"Not exactly, Seth," said Mr. Levine. "Reagan's 'neutrality' offended a lot of us. But what happened when average guys like you and me questioned Reagan's dealings with the apartheid regime?"

"Congress sanctioned South Africa," Drew said.

"So how could people like us support the student protesters in China?"

"Boycott Chinese products," said Terrence.

"People like you and I can conduct foreign policy?" Mr. Levine asked.

"Right," said Terrence.

Mr. Levine grabbed a dusty eraser and flung it at a poster on the wall behind him:

> ## "Do you want to know who you are? Don't ask. Act! Action will delineate and define you."
> ### -THOMAS JEFFERSON

"Americans don't have to be neutral even when our government attempts to be?" Mr. Levine asked.

"No," said most of the class. Mr. Levine gazed around the room until everyone made full eye contact.

"You're damn right we don't!" he shouted. He bounced on his heels. "Americans live in the oldest democracy and the richest country on the globe. Do you have any idea what happens when people like you and me get really, really pissed off?" He pointed at Quinn's raised hand.

"We change the world."

Seth waited for Quinn outside class. They walked in silence to a low-traffic west entrance. When the coast was clear, Seth pulled her into a quiet corner of the foyer.

"I heard what you said at prom," he said, "Even though you were being super bossy and your timing sucked." She started to say something, but he stopped her. "You're right that part of me does think that I only deserve what I already have—not what I actually want. So thanks for that."

"I'm sorry I was such a bitch. I got so nervous. I should never have dragged you there."

"In my house you're not allowed to say *bitch*. It's a gendered slam. You weren't a bitch. You were an asshole."

Quinn laughed. "Yes. Again, sorry about that."

"I kind of love fighting with you," Seth admitted.

"That's messed up."

"What I mean is, I like it that—even when you act like an asshole—you respect me enough to disagree with me. You assume I'm smart and strong enough to handle it."

"Well, I do. You are." She kissed him. He grinned.

"Or maybe that's not it at all. Maybe I just like this part. It's like makeup sex without the sex."

"We should talk about that sometime."

"I'm listening." He grinned for a second before realizing he'd be late for work if he didn't get home to his mom right now. "Okay, actually, I'm not. I have to get going. But maybe this weekend we could discuss my permanent hard-on situation?"

He had fallen in love with Quinn. Her giggle carried him home.

CHAPTER 24
REVOLUTION

His mom called July "the dead season," when the morning dew on the grass made promises it couldn't keep. Each day flattened like a hot bike tire. The sun perched at what felt like high noon for eight hours a day. The nights hung on to the swampy heat with about as much reprieve as a terrarium.

"Mom, can you help me with something?" Seth yelled as he climbed the basement stairs. Fatigue hit him as soon as he reached the humid kitchen. It was only eight o'clock in the morning.

"Sure, honey," she called faintly from her bedroom. Seth flipped on the air conditioner in the dining room window. It took forever to get going in the mornings but ate too much electricity to justify running it through the night.

His hands trembled as he set the University of Nebraska-Lincoln, application materials and Mr. Levine's financial aid forms on the dining room table. The chances of this being a casual conversation were not so great, but he'd been putting it off now for weeks.

He and Quinn had walked together at graduation and had managed to go to a couple of parties as a couple without causing any scenes. Now that she had a job, too, though, they only saw each other a few times a week. Days were whipping by as if the world had started spinning faster. If he didn't act now he felt like he'd wake up tomorrow at age fifty with a bad back and sawdust in his hair.

As he walked into his mom's bedroom, she was trying to push herself up with her strong arm into a sitting position. Her pallid face and fake smile told him everything. Sometimes the MS lunged at her in her sleep to deliver a fresh beating. The doctor called it an "acceleration," the euphemism a total insult to the person on the receiving end.

"Bad night, huh?" Seth pushed a cat out of the way and sat on the end of her bed. Clearly, their conversation would have to wait. Again.

"Hurts." Seth saw the tears well in her eyes as she tried to push herself up farther on her stack of crushed pillows. He rubbed one of her aching legs as if to distract them both. "Let's talk about you," she said, forcing another smile and roughly wiping her eyes with a fist. "I'm already sick of myself."

"That's okay. Nothing to tell." Seth cast his eyes at the floor.

She coughed and cleared her throat. "Would you snag me some coffee, beautiful?" she croaked. "I could use a hit."

"Sure." He trudged to the kitchen and mixed a teaspoon of instant coffee in a mug of hot tap water. At the side of her bed, he held it steady for her as she slowly wrapped her stronger hand around it. She took a couple of long swallows and popped a pain pill. She drank again.

"You said you needed my help? That'd be a nice change of

pace." He tried to think of a lie but drew a blank. His mom noticed. She ditched her cheerful act. "Spill it, kid."

He smelled wisps of sulfur-smelling breeze creeping through the open screens. The kids next door had discovered bottle rockets; they'd operated a launch pad in their front yard for this whole week before the Fourth of July. Seth got up to close the windows. He sat back down.

"I want to go to the U," he blurted. He watched his mom's face. He wished he'd started this conversation a year ago instead of wasting precious time. His mom spilled some coffee down her nightgown and onto the worn sheet. Seth mopped it up with a wad of Kleenex.

"Now?"

"At the beginning of the semester next year."

"Honey," she murmured. "The timing isn't that great." She put her clawed right hand on top of his. Seth didn't move. Would the answer have been different if he'd asked the question yesterday or a year ago? He cleared his throat as the neighbor kid set off another volley of firecrackers. Seth knew he'd find half the spent red spindles in their own backyard.

"When do you think the timing would be better?" he asked a little more gruffly than he'd meant.

His mom's sympathetic smile faded. Hurt crept into her eyes. "When we have some savings?"

"We're never going to have any savings." His mom flinched. "But Mr. Levine thinks I'm scholarship material. He said he could help me with the paperwork." His mom used to talk about all the scholarships he'd be eligible for. When exactly had she stopped? When had he let himself stop dreaming? Seth pressed his lips together and waited for her to act like a parent. Instead, she exploded.

"Jesus, Seth! Why are you doing this? Why are you pushing this now? You have lots of time." In theory, this was true. But once they got used to his full-time earnings next year, he knew it would never make sense for him to dial back to earning less. He went on the offensive.

"You don't want me to go to college."

"I do! Of course I do. I just . . . God, I need you here. I'm a fucking mess. I feel horrible thinking it—let alone saying it out loud—but there it is. You deserve a college education. You've worked hard for it. I really, really want that for you. But I admit it. The idea scares the hell out of me. Just let me think about it, okay?"

"Maybe we could apply for another health aide?" A year ago, Seth had looked into home health care. The county had sent over a bustling woman in white polyester who'd patronized his mom with pep talks about mind over matter, like MS could be cured with a good mood.

"Oh, God. That bitch was such a bust," his mom said, shaking her head. "When she wasn't congratulating herself for inflicting her good deeds on me, she was reading my mail." That arrangement had lasted nine days.

"You're not supposed to say *bitch*."

"Right. Asshole then."

"Much better. Nice, Mom." He smiled.

"But seriously, Seth. You would totally qualify for a college scholarship. And I'll be so happy when you're on your way. But it's the wrong time. Scholarships won't pay for a ramp and bathroom rails. We have to get squared away first."

"Don't forget the medications and the hospital stays," Seth spat. He hadn't realized how close to the surface his anger lurked. "Mom, we'll never get 'squared away'! That's what I'm saying. If I wait until we're 'ready,' I'll miss my chance."

His mom threw up her arms—or tried to, anyway. "Do it then. No one wants you to go to college more than I do."

Seth crossed his arms. "Really? You don't act like it."

She glared at him. Then she went for his jugular. "Going to college still won't make you a long-term prospect for Quinn Ganey. I can see it coming from a mile away. Your rich little girlfriend is getting you all puffed up to be good enough for her. But soon—you watch—she's outta here." Seth looked her in the eye.

"Okay, Mom. Maybe she will blow me off. She's definitely not perfect. But you know what? She told me that I'm not the only one holding me back. And do you know what? She's right." A faint cloud of blue smoke drifted by their side window now from one of those pointless ten-cent smoke bombs. His mom opened her mouth to retaliate and closed it. He saw the grim truth of his words sink in. "Do you actually think I'd be disappointed that I have a four-year degree?" he persisted. "How many people do you know who regret going to college? And like you keep saying, there are all kinds of scholarships and grants for people like me."

Her eyes narrowed. "And how would you describe 'a person like you,' Seth? You think your life is rough?"

Seth leaped to his feet and stood over her. "What the hell

do you know about my life, Mom? You think it's hard being in a wheelchair at age forty-two? Try being tethered to the same wheelchair at seventeen! Try seeing the girl you love not only leave town, but outgrow you and evolve beyond you!"

His mom flinched at the word *love*. Her little body trembled as she shook her crumpled hand at him. "What about being widowed at age twenty-five and raising a baby by yourself?" she shouted. "Or getting a landscaping certificate, staying sober, giving up your social life, and still not being able to pay for groceries? Try being scared every moment of your life. Try hanging on to what's 'normal' while knowing 'normal' will disappear again any minute! Do you have any idea what it feels like to have your own body betray you and have God slap you down each time you pick yourself up?"

Seth sat back down. She was right. What kind of idiot expected fairness? What single moment of their lives so far had ever led him to believe that someday it might all work out? He tried to repack his resentment.

"No. Of course I don't," he said. He reached for her hands. Her eyes welled with tears. He passed her another Kleenex as her nose started to run. She leaned back in her chair, gray with exhaustion.

Seth had to run the six blocks to work. When he got home, he helped his mom and made dinner in silence. He spent the evening staring at the ceiling of his bedroom, wishing he'd never opened his big fat mouth. At about ten o'clock, the city's siren warned its denizens to find shelter. He ran upstairs.

"C'mon, Dorothy," Seth told his mom as he pushed her in her chair from her bedroom to the frame of the kitchen door. Her legs still hurt, but she stood up and shuffled over to peer out the kitchen window and admire the dark clouds clumped like boulders over the horizon. The sky had a fake quality, like a set for a junior high musical. The clouds' dark shadows contrasted with the eerie yellow light. After slowly descending the basement stairs, the two of them watched as much television as they could stand before lying on his bed, feeling thunder rattle their teeth. In the end, only a rainstorm touched ground. It lifted by early morning, leaving behind a regular sunrise, as if they hadn't nearly gotten spun to Oz. People referred to this corner of Nebraska as Tornado Alley; the wide-open plains just beyond downtown seemed specially designed to help regular wind speed up and wreak havoc.

When they woke up to the orange rays, Seth buckled the brace on his mom's leg and helped her stand. She began most days walking before fatigue forced her back into her chair. Today she had to sit back down twice on his bed, swearing softly. Her nightgown smelled sour; Seth put laundry on his mental to-do list.

Yesterday's depressing stalemate dissolved back into the tedium of their daily routine. They stuck to their plan to visit the garden store before Seth's shift at the lumberyard. Last week, he'd pried their grubby window boxes off their nails. He'd brought them inside for his mom. Playing in the dirt again—even if it was only scraping the spent soil into a trash can—had made her loud and playful. Seth wished he could bottle those bursts of happiness and uncork them on grimmer days like this one.

They Handi-Vanned to Campbell's Nursery. Seth alternated

between pushing his mom's chair and pushing a cart. She relaxed in the earthy-smelling humidity. They'd be okay: forgiving each other was something they did a lot.

He'd forgotten Quinn was working today. He sneaked up behind her and untied her green apron as she misted a tray of succulents.

She turned around. When she saw it was him, she lit up. Then she misted his face. She waved at his mom who sat in the aisle a few feet back. "Hi, Debbie. What are you getting?" Typically, his mom went for sophisticated blends of ferns and waxy ivy with blue forget-me-nots or white impatiens. Now she showed Quinn the contenders in her lap. They had all the subtlety of a pep rally, like she planned to cram every cheerful flower she'd ever seen—including hot-pink zinnias—into their three window boxes. "Let me get you a better one of those zinnias," Quinn said. "I watered a bunch a minute ago. Be right back." They waited for her.

"She's crazy about you, Seth," his mom murmured.

"You think?" he asked. She nodded.

Quinn came back with a bushier six-pack of zinnia seedlings. She squatted down by his mom's chair and tucked it into the crook of her weaker arm.

"Mom," Seth joked as he watched them together, "I'm not sure I'm man enough to have Barbie window boxes."

"If anyone is man enough for Barbie pink, it's you," his mom said. "Right, Quinn?"

"Definitely," said Quinn. "You want me to mist his face again while he thinks about it?"

"Good idea," said Debbie.

At home, Seth rolled her chair up to the dining room table. After piling the plants, window boxes, bag of potting soil, and a half-full watering can within his reach, he went outside to finish the prep work around the windows. He brushed off the drip-dried rain mud. The new hook-and-eye hardware was easy to screw into the weathered wood.

Back inside, his mom had finished repotting and was sitting back—wiped out—in her chair. Seth hoisted a window box off the table. They were heavy. He should have hung them up before letting his mom pour in a gallon of water and Miracle-Gro. He saw the expression on her face and put the box back down.

"Bathroom?" he asked her.

"Yes. Then bed," she said, closing her eyes for a moment. Seth pulled back her chair from the table and pushed it to the bathroom doorframe. He straightened and locked her leg brace.

"Don't you have to take a college entrance exam or something first?" she asked, taking Seth's arm to help her stand. Her voice sounded high, almost giddy. She started shuffling forward at twice her normal pace. Seth looked at her sideways. He cleared his dry throat and tried to sound casual.

"I did. I'm in the top five percent."

His mom smiled. It spread to her eyes. "Fill out that application, genius boy."

"You think?" Seth studied the hallway carpet.

"I do. You're right. You need to get ready for your life. I'm happy for you. We'll be fine."

"I didn't mean that I don't have a life now."

She hugged him with her head on his chest. "It's okay, honey.

Okay? We'll both be fine." At that moment, Seth could have used a couple of leg braces himself. His mom repeated, "We'll both be fine."

CHAPTER 25
WORLD WAR III

White geraniums now took over the terra-cotta pot on the front porch that in June had held Quinn's dad's purple and yellow pansies. With plenty of water and some shade from the porch, they'd make it through the furnace of July and August. Nebraska summers caused your hair to stick to your neck and made you want to whine like a three-year-old. Quinn pinched off a juicy, fuzzy leaf at the base of one plant and held it to her nose. Its astringent scent cooled and calmed her.

She smelled the citrus before she found her mom standing at the kitchen island, sectioning grapefruit for a lettuce salad. Her mom still wore the belted orange silk dress that made her olive skin and brown eyes glow. Her dad stood on the opposite side of the counter in his work clothes. He waved a greeting while snitching grapefruit out of the salad. Her mom smiled at Quinn as she lifted the salad bowl out of her dad's reach and set it on the counter behind her.

Quinn's dad mixed cocktails for her mom and himself and turned the radio on to NPR. Quinn poured herself a glass of orange juice and retreated to the hard-tiled breakfast nook with the newspaper. The tiny room with its two powerful air vents felt like a deep freeze.

The newspaper's front page headline said, "*Webster* Decision Weakens *Roe v. Wade.*" Quinn leaned in to read the article as her dad set down his vodka tonic by the seat next to her. He hung his suit jacket carefully over the back of the chair. They heard her mom switch the radio to KFMQ classic rock in the adjoining room and turn up the volume. He sniffed. His eyes twinkled.

"Are you messing with my geraniums again?" he asked. Quinn made her face solemn and gazed up at him through her eyelashes. Maybe they were getting back to normal.

"Only this one time."

He shook his head at her. "Uh-huh. Last year, they looked like palm trees by September." He stretched his arms by hanging on to the top of the doorway and letting his body weight pull him forward.

"I haven't seen Trish around in a while. Are you two okay?" An olive branch.

"Trish doesn't like Seth." Quinn and Trish weren't ignoring each other or anything: they just hadn't gone out of their way to talk since prom. But it was more than that, Quinn realized. The relationship had stopped growing somewhere back in ninth grade. She'd gotten stuck in a role that didn't fit her anymore. Maybe going to separate colleges would help them find their way back to each other. Or maybe it wouldn't.

"Maybe it's like the clubs we talked about. Some people only know who they are by pointing a finger at who they aren't. I'm sure she'll find her way." Quinn nodded, grateful, for once, for one of his speeches. She saw him glance at the headline.

"I saw that, too," he said, nodding at it.

"I've only read a paragraph." Pointedly, she went back to reading.

"The Supreme Court decided to restrict abortion," he said. "You know your mother and I are pro-choice, right? We believe the government should stay out of our personal lives."

Quinn nodded. That made three of them. Her dad stood, leaning now on the back of the breakfast chair.

"Missouri passed a law a while back that restricted abortion. The lower courts tossed it out as being an 'undue burden,' but it ended up going all the way to the Supreme Court. They're trying to roll back *Roe v. Wade.*"

"I know." Quinn began reading the article again, hoping he'd take the hint. But he was deaf to her body language.

"This *Webster* decision makes it okay for other states to pass new restrictions." He walked back to the cupboard and found the Wheat Thins. He munched a few. Quinn's mom came around the corner and wiped her hands on a linen tea towel. Her nails sported a shiny double coat of maroon polish.

"It also means that if the government pays for your health care, you can't get an abortion at all," she said quietly. Quinn glanced back down at the newspaper. Getting an abortion was already an undue burden; she'd been a nervous, lonely, nauseated fucking mess. She'd talked about sex with strangers, traveled two hours, and had had surgery and a day of bad cramps. And she'd paid two hundred fifty dollars in cash for the privilege.

"I think I'm a Democrat," Quinn blurted. Her heart thudded

like she'd just seen a speeding locomotive in her rearview mirror. A corner of her mom's mouth twitched upward. Her dad put on his patient neutral face and sat down in his chair.

"Why's that?" He reached again into the box of crackers.

"Because this . . ." Quinn read the headline again, "*Webster* decision is stupid."

"The Republican Party didn't make the decision, Ace. The Supreme Court did." Quinn heard her mom go back to slicing carrots in the next room. The angry crack in the sliding glass door caught her eye. It made her feel stupid all over again. It had meandered up about ten inches toward the middle of the pane as if it hadn't decided whether or not to stop.

"I know, but—"

"This is how a democracy works, Quinn. We swing back and forth between liberalism and conservatism." Her father rocked his chair onto its back legs. His detached calm made her feel—as usual—slightly hysterical. She moved aside her orange juice with shaky fingers.

"But that doesn't mean I have to go along with it." Her mom's carrot chopping slowed on the other side of the doorway. All the gritty emotions from the last couple of months pinged and clawed at Quinn's thin composure. "I mean, people like Seth and his mom are even poorer than they used to be. And now Republicans are trying to water down *Roe v. Wade*." If Mr. Levine were here, she knew he'd back her up on this. She saw a tiny smile on her dad's face.

Her dad let the front legs of the chair touch the floor again. "You're annoyed. And you're right. In a conservative climate, you'd think that it would be easier—not harder—to make a personal decision like that." He wasn't smiling now. Maybe she'd gotten to him and she could back down. "But on balance our freedoms are safest when states have more power than the federal government."

Quinn could still taste the fear of walking across that clinic parking lot, of the panic that the protesters might actually block the door. Would they have stopped them if Seth hadn't shown up? Which side did the law protect? She didn't even know.

"You mean like with slave states and free states?" she demanded.

Her dad thunked down his drink and sighed. "You make a good point, Quinn. Well done. But that was over a hundred years ago. Times have changed. Just because you've started to pay attention doesn't mean you have it all figured out. You don't."

Now he seemed irritated. He jabbed the article with his finger for emphasis.

"Please remember that being in love with Seth doesn't make you poor or virtuous by association. You're not an authority on single mothers or the disabled or fatherless children or on how to solve their problems." Was she in love with Seth? And what did he have to do with this conversation? "Who do you think pays for the government handouts that create a cycle of dependence? I do. The only thing that helps everyone is a healthy economy."

"But, Dad, even in a good economy, some people still go hungry. That means there's something wrong with the system. Seth isn't even sure he can go to college, because he has to help support his mom." Quinn needed her dad to know—like she knew—that no one deserved to be miserable.

"Quinn, even in a wealthy country like ours, there will always be poor, disabled and hungry people. My earliest memories are of the Depression. Thanks to Social Security, we can now keep old people from dying in poverty. But when bureaucracies try to do more than the bare minimum, they make a damned mess out of it." He jingled the change in his pockets. "Private charity makes welfare unnecessary. Or at least it should. Your mother gives to the battered women's shelter. I run a private foundation. We help stock the food bank. We know better than Congress how to help out and where help is needed."

Quinn took a deep breath. She should try humor, she knew, to diffuse this. But she couldn't find any.

"People helping their neighbors *should* take away the need for a safety net. But it isn't working. Seth and Debbie are on welfare, and they're still not safe."

"Yes, they are, Quinn," her dad said gently. "They're struggling. They lead a tough existence. But our safety nets do keep them from being homeless or starving. They have hard lives, as many—most—people do, but they are safe." She scowled. For a generous person, he could be heartless. "At the end of the day, Americans' individual freedom—within the law—trumps the right of the government to get in our business." The nearby vegetable chopping stilled. For the first time in her life, Quinn saw a flaw in her father's logic. She pounced on it.

"What about now? Is taking away my right to a legal abortion 'protecting my individual freedom'?" Her dad flinched. "It sounds more like Jim Crow to me."

"You're right about that, Quinn," he said. "You could view this as another Jim Crow issue—maybe individuals' freedom in this case would be best served by a strong federal law."

Quinn couldn't believe it; her dad had conceded a point. "So you agree with me that conservatives are caving in to the religious wackos?"

"I wouldn't go that far. Keeping religion out of government is essential. But we're simply in the middle of a typical historical pattern." Quinn rolled her eyes on the inside. "When American technology leaps forward like it is right now, a religious revival always follows. We've seen it twice already in our history. Change is scary. When people fear change, they lean harder on religion. Throw in Bill Gates and a new millennium, and paranoid people go nuts. That's all that this current nonsense amounts to."

"You don't worry about peoples' rights disappearing in the meantime?"

"It'll blow over."

Her mom came around the corner, wielding a zucchini in one hand and a vegetable peeler in the other.

"Tom," she said, "can you imagine the uproar if the Supreme Court had made it harder this week for wealthy men to vote?"

"Evelyn, please."

"What?" Her mom pressed her lips together and put the zucchini into the same hand as the vegetable peeler as she waited for him to reply.

"This isn't about the right to vote," he said.

"Thank you, Professor," she said sarcastically. "But Quinn is right. If the courts made it harder to buy a hunting rifle, you'd hardly sit there saying, 'It'll blow over.'"

Her dad glanced at Quinn and then back at her mom as if to show to an invisible audience the firing squad he faced. "Evelyn, where did this come from?" he tried to laugh. "Can't you tell I'm on your side?"

Quinn's mom leaned toward the breakfast table and smacked the open newspaper. "What I see, Tom Ganey, is a"—she glanced at Quinn—"*man* who thinks that being pro-choice is being on his wife and daughters' 'side.' I see someone who's not as philosophically pure as he thinks he is."

He blinked. "I beg your pardon?"

"You think of democracy as some grand theory concocted by your Founding Father pals," she said, drawing circles in the air. "But you only connect the dots to right now in 1989 when it suits you. You argue for small government and the rights of the individual. But when you view my right—Quinn's right—to have an abortion, you only see a pesky side issue." She stood up straight again. "Living, breathing democracy is messy, Tom. You don't get to do it from your leather office chair." She stopped to catch Quinn's eye—woman-to-woman—before walking out of the kitchen.

Her father stood up, screeching the floor with the chair. He took his time fixing himself another drink. Quinn sat there, slowly circling the rim of her juice glass with her fingertip.

"Quinn, I hope you know that I'm not observing the *Webster* decision from the sidelines. I'm saying that it's merely one court decision, not a Congressional tidal wave. Women can still get abortions. There's no reason to get hysterical." His sexist choice of words was the last straw.

"Mom's right," Quinn said, standing up quietly.

"Your mother is being emotional," he said, sipping his drink.

"Yes, Dad, she is." For all these years, Quinn had debated her father on his terms. "But having emotions doesn't keep you from developing fully formed opinions. And people get emotional about things that are personal." He tried to interrupt her, but she cut him off. "This is about people in power—people like you—looking the other way and telling the rest of us to suck it up while our civil rights disappear. You've dropped the ball, Dad, and you don't even know it."

Through the glass door, Quinn saw some brave gasps of color in the backyard. A dark purple delphinium had shocked them all that summer by blooming next to the deck after two years of placidly doing nothing.

"I think you're letting your politically correct new friends affect your judgment," her dad said.

Quinn had spent her whole life worrying about appearing to lose her judgment. She tended to tread softly, carefully paying her dues to join her dad's club. But she didn't want to be in that club anymore.

"Dad," she said, "If you think you're neutral, you're kidding yourself." He started to respond, but again Quinn talked over him. "You know what they call people who believe they're neutral and think the rest of us are special interest groups?"

"Quinn!" her dad warned.

"They call them bigots!"

They stared at each other. His eyes snapped as he stood up

and pointed a shaking finger at her. He opened his mouth to yell back and . . . changed his mind. He let out a long, quiet breath before yanking his jacket from the back of the chair and leaving the room.

Quinn rode a wave of nausea. She used to think the worst thing would be for him to lose respect for her. Now she realized—after pushing her hero off his pedestal—that her losing respect for him was way worse.

She found her mom sitting on the front porch, fanning herself with some junk mail. Quinn sat next to her on the cold cement slab.

"I don't care what Newt What's-His-Name says," her mom said. "True conservatives like your dad and me stay out of people's business because we assume they can think and provide for themselves. And we work in our own communities to help those who can't." Quinn started to speak, but her mom gestured to let her finish. "Your dad is definitely guilty of being a privileged white male. He likes the view from where he sits. And who wouldn't? But he's not some fascist jerk, Quinn. One of my college roommates went to Chicago for an illegal abortion before *Roe* and died. Died! Your dad knows that."

She looked into Quinn's eyes to make sure she understood.

"This afternoon was not your dad's finest hour. But you need to know that if push came to shove, he'd go to the mat for legal abortion, not only because he has two daughters and a wife, but because he's a true conservative. Personal freedom is everything." Quinn pinched off a geranium leaf and started folding the edges. "Okay?" her mom asked, brushing off her backside.

"Okay," Quinn said.

But it wasn't.

CHAPTER 26
RED DAWN

The next Saturday, Quinn picked up Seth from the lumber-yard. They splurged on ingredients for BLTs, Tater Tots, and fresh peaches—his mom's favorites—at Ideal grocery before heading to his house to make dinner.

The house looked like shit, Seth realized. He sized up the bright orange and fuchsia flowers in his mom's window boxes as he and Quinn each carried a grocery bag up to the front porch. The flowers made the rest of the house seem grubbier in comparison.

Seth needed to get Quinn alone. Last night he'd canceled their plans to picnic at Holmes Lake; his mom couldn't get ahead of the pain. Quinn joked that all they'd missed out on was a bunch of mosquitoes, but he'd been looking forward to several hours of fooling around on a blanket under the stars.

He tried to let go of Quinn's hand to get his keys out of his pocket. She wouldn't let him. She laughed as he pretended to be annoyed and shook her off. He squeezed her now-tickling fingers together as he tried again to reach for his keys. Her easy laughter smoothed his nerves.

He loved her. He'd come close last weekend to blurting it, but then chickened out. Technically, he'd offered up his whole heart before—in writing—and had gotten his ass kicked.

Since the trip to the gardening store, Seth had been studying the UNL application materials and figuring out how to enroll for the second semester. He hoped his mom might even help him tonight with the financial aid forms if her good mood still held.

He got the door unlocked. He laughed as Quinn rubbed his ribs with her knuckles. He turned back to the porch to get the mail. The Social Security check—the last one they'd get—sat on top of the stack. He'd think about that later.

He closed the storm door and jostled Quinn into the living room. He shushed her, though, when he saw the empty space where his mom usually sat. Late-afternoon quiet blanketed the house. Good. His mom's rare naps helped her sleep better at night. Relaxing a little helped her relax even more, which often helped with the pain. Better yet, he had Quinn to himself now.

He turned to her. He held her waist with the hand holding the mail and pulled her shoulders close with his other arm. He kissed her long and slow, sucking on the tip of her tongue. She answered with something between a sigh and a moan, pressing closer. He needed to check his mom, then get Quinn to his room. Now.

He pulled away. Quinn pretended to pout as he gestured for her to sit between Sid Not-So-Vicious and Nancy, who curled up on the sofa like two fuzzy donuts, one on each cushion. The dried soil and vermiculite mess still waited for him under the dining room table. He tiptoed through to his mom's bedroom.

She snoozed on her back with her hair cushioning her turned

head, a thick purple and gray yoga bolster under her knees. Seth straightened the covers over her tiny body. The Indian batik on the thin bedspread had faded from fierce maroon to an incongruously sweet magenta. The dark circles under her eyes got more bruised-looking every day, but the chronic anxiety line between her brows had faded as she slept. He checked her cluttered bedside table for dirty dishes, lifting an empty water glass from a small mountain of used Kleenexes.

A capless, empty prescription bottle lurked behind the faint water ring left by the glass. Yesterday it had been half-full. Seth spun around. He pressed sweaty fingers against her cool neck, trying but failing to find a pulse. He watched her, waiting for her chest to rise and fall. Nothing.

"What's your worst fear?" Aunt Gail had asked her during that visit to Des Moines. His mom had replied, "That I'll wake up one day and realize I'm too helpless to kill myself."

Seth bent his knees slowly and groped for the edge of the mattress behind him. The box spring squeaked when he sat but didn't offer any real resistance. He pulled back the batik spread. His mom's arms seemed strangely loose now at her sides, the freckles starker now against her bloodless forearms. Had she purposely uncurled her right hand as the painkillers had kicked in, or had death given her this small reprieve? He put his palms on his knees, forcing himself to draw breaths. The stillness of the warm room cupped him like a tiny, downy nest. He put a tanned hand on his mom's white one, squeezing it to stave off the creeping chill.

So much for being honest. So much for letting down his guard around her for five fucking minutes. He'd blown it.

No, she'd blown it. Seth clenched his jaw. He let go of his mom's still-pliant hand. He pressed his thumb and fingers to his prickling eyes.

"No," he rasped. He squeezed his eyes closed. What a bitch. What. A. Fucking. Bitch. Seth's tears dripped onto his sawdusty Levi's: five drops, eight, twelve. He stood and grabbed a Kleenex off the painted dresser. He leaned against the wall above it with both palms. What the hell was he supposed to do now? He hung his head and spilled more tears onto the dresser's dusty surface. The dust only partially absorbed the wet drops, forming a weak, salty mud.

He blew his nose. He turned and leaned against the dresser. Time creaked. He inventoried the four walls of his mom's existence. "Fuck the Draft," shouted an old, cheaply framed poster. Plastic trays of salmon-colored flowers hogged the length of both windowsills. They sagged slightly where the edges overlapped the varnished wood. The five-year-old clematis vine outside now nearly reached the middle of one window, offering up its purple blooms. His mom had covered nearly all the other surfaces in woven South American blankets and placemats. Seth smiled in spite of himself at the ugly metal trash can they'd decorated together a decade ago. They'd used greeting cards and an unwieldy roll of sticky laminating paper.

A square photo showed his uniformed dad standing outside a building, holding Seth's infant self. It leaned in its tiny frame against the lamp on his mom's bedside table. He picked up the photo. His dad seemed so young, was so young. He hadn't been much older than Seth when he'd died. As Seth approached him in age, he realized he'd started thinking of his dad as Jeff. The older he got, the less angry he was about his dad's sudden exit. It wasn't Jeff's fault. Maybe he'd wanted to be a father as much as Seth had wanted to have one. Seth pitied the handsome young guy in the photo who had just barely started living.

The folded note waited for him, wedged behind the picture frame. Seth leaned over slowly and pinched it between his thumb and finger. His mom's huge scrawls took up three one-sided pages of spiral notebook paper, sliding in some places to the paper's shaggy edge. It would have taken her hours.

July 15, 1989

Dear Seth,

You must be shocked and furious and sad. I'm sorry.

You may not believe this (or care right now), but I'm happy. I'm free. I'm ready to die.

I hate the fear that's taken over my life. I'm tired of never having a state of "normal." Before MS, I had no idea how much I counted on being whole and healthy. Maybe someday you'll appreciate that some things really are worse than death: things like living a fourth of a life and watching my son settle for the same.

For what it's worth, I did ask my doctor about the endgame and whether he could help. What I learned is that not only is assisted suicide a crime, living wills aren't even legal in Nebraska. I can't bear the idea of someone

making me live longer than I want to simply because oth-
er people fear death. I have to take charge while I still
can.

I think you know deep down that I've been planning
this. Nothing you did or didn't do caused it. Nothing
you did or didn't do could have prevented it. Our recent
argument only brought me clarity, after weeks of pain
and ambivalence. I'm grateful for it. I've been waiting
for you to make your own way, I guess. I realize now how
hard I've also been trying to stop you. It was a relief when
you made me realize this. The pace of this disease beats
me down as much as the pain and fatigue do. I never
get my bearings. I never get to reflect on what's right in
front of me.

Watching you stand up for yourself showed me that
I'd already done what I've been desperate to do: I've
raised a son who can survive without me. This hurts. It
also makes me proud. I've been a flawed but good moth-
er: at seventeen, you're already the kind of person I hoped
you would become. I know I'm not perfect. Maybe I'm
even the coward who left early so she wouldn't get left
behind. But at the end of the day, I've raised a good man.

Remember crying into our popcorn over Terms of
Endearment? *Remember when Debra Winger tells her*
moody son on her deathbed that she knows he loves her?
Well, I do. I know you love me. I also know you resent me
sometimes and that you hate my MS. It's okay, beautiful.

You might also feel some relief right now. That's fine, too. Anyone in your reeking Converse shoes would feel the same way. ☺

Being your mother has been the greatest joy of my life. You wore me out when you were a toddler. I didn't know a kid could run that much. You were shy and kind in grade school, my little man. Being a mom has made me so frigging responsible I hardly recognize myself. Raising someone I admire as much as you has made me a better person. I'm proud of both of us.

Please live your big, amazing life, Seth, knowing that I lived mine as big and as amazingly as I could. I love you so much.

Mom

The last page dangled from his fingers. He folded it with the others. He leaned over and perched the letter against the lamp again. There were probably official things you were supposed to do when someone died. He should call 911 or something. Right now, though, his body would only do one thing. Seth stumbled to the other side of the bed. He curled himself around his mom. He inhaled the living smell of shampoo in her hair. He didn't have to pretend for her anymore that everything was okay. It wasn't. He didn't have to take one more for the team. There was no team. The only thing to do right now was to cry. A floorboard creaked.

"Seth?"

He jumped. He'd forgotten about Quinn. He lifted his head

to look at her wide-eyed but stayed next to his mom. "She's dead."

Quinn's gaze swerved to his mom's face and back to his.

"Overdose," he said.

Tears blurred Quinn's blue eyes. They streamed across her cheeks and dripped down her neck. She let them for a minute before pressing her face against the crook of her bare arm. As he closed his eyes, he heard her kick off her shoes and walk around the end of the bed. She laid down behind him and molded her warm body around his back, resting her hand on top of his on top of his mom's.

Sid Not-So-Vicious yawned a yowl from the hallway before strolling in and spotting a place on the bed to land. He hopped up next to his mom's feet and picked his way over to Seth and Quinn. Sid arranged himself—as only a cat would—in an orange disc pressed to the bottoms of Seth's feet. Seth breathed deeper still as gravity slightly loosened its pull. Sandwiched here between life and death, Seth felt light and strange. Strangely safe.

An hour later, he sat up. Quinn did the same as he staggered to the bathroom. He washed his face and found his reflection in the mirror. The man staring back at him seemed to know what to do. He called 911. He called his aunt and Mr. Levine. Quinn called her parents. She held Seth's hand as they stood in the doorway. Together they waited as the paramedics brought their stretcher up to the house.

CHAPTER 27
THE DAY AFTER

Seth leaned against the sink in his kitchen, tearing open Quinn's letter.

July 18, 1989

Dear Seth,

Mom and I just got home from bringing you Daylight Donuts. (Next time we'll get more of the maple long johns. Who knew anyone actually liked those things?) Your aunt Gail is really nice. Lee is cool, too, even though he kicked my butt in driveway basketball.

I'm writing you this letter because it makes me feel like I'm doing something. I've never been close to someone who's lost a parent. I don't know how to act or what to say. Here goes:

I'm so sorry. I'm sorry for your loss. I'm sorry for her pain. I'm sorry for yours.

I'm also sorry for acting like a spoiled brat know-it-all

about your life with your mom. In my head, I made her the bad guy, like she was trying to drag you down. I was a moron. I'm sorry for trying to put myself in the middle of a situation that was none of my business. Thank you for showing me her note. It made me happy for you that you had such a great mom. And it made me sad for myself that I didn't know her better.

My dad asks about you all the time. (I'm still totally pissed at him but have to admit he's being super nice.) I'll see you tomorrow (and the next day and the next day . . .).

Love,

Quinn

Dear Quinn,

You think you don't know what to do or say, but you do. Thanks for showing up. Thanks for letting me cry on you. Thanks for figuring out how to use our relic of a washing machine and doing all the laundry. That was great. Aunt Gail says thanks, too.

Speaking of showing up, I looked out the window a few hours ago and your dad was mowing our lawn. Isn't he the guy who landscaped your whole front yard so he'd never have to push a mower? When I went out to talk to him, he told me he was sorry he'd never met my mom. When I told him about the pain she'd been in and how it had been getting worse, do you know what he said? He said, "I can't imagine how hard this must be for you, but if I were in your mom's position, I would have done the same thing." In a messed up sort of way, it made me feel better.

Thanks for what you said about my mom. You may have noticed that I'm not perfect either. We can be fuck-ups together, okay?

I'm going through my mom's things and am a total head case. One minute I'm admiring her campaign button collection. The next minute I'm blubbering over a Tootsie Roll wrapper on her closet floor. I found a complete landscape design that she'd made for our yard and cried over it for an hour. Then I get a letter from my girlfriend and I'm a) happier than I've ever been, and b) feeling guilty about not feeling miserable.

See you in, like, five minutes.

Love,

Seth

He borrowed a suit from Lee for his mom's funeral. About thirty pairs of eyes—including relatives' and his mom's former coworkers'—offered him sympathy as he gave a short eulogy. Quinn sat with her mother and father. Mr. Levine sat with Terrence, Michelle, and Ilene. Having all these people here made him realize he wasn't nearly as alone in the world as he had sometimes felt. Reading straight from his handwritten notes helped him not puke. He was pretty sure his mom would have liked it. She definitely would have liked the fact that her Barbie-pink window boxes served as floral arrangements. He was man enough for that.

He and Quinn stood talking to Mr. Levine afterward in an alcove of the funeral home lobby. Mr. Levine seemed to get it that Seth wanted to be distracted, not pitied. They talked about the Chinese soldiers mowing down the prodemocracy student protesters and how Chinese teenagers with fax machines had spread the news to the world. Seth hadn't even heard that Poland had held its first free election after over forty years of Soviet rule.

"They have a lot to look forward to," Mr. Levine said, "but this must be a scary time." He squeezed Seth's shoulder as he said this.

"I did hear that the Supreme Court ruled that flag burning counted as 'free speech.' I love all the conservative outrage. Good thing we're starting 'a new world order' with our eye on the ball, right?" Seth cracked this joke right as Mr. Ganey strolled over. Seth saw Quinn tense up.

"Are we talking about flag burning?" Mr. Ganey asked, reaching out to shake Mr. Levine's hand.

"We are," said Mr. Levine, returning the gesture. "What do you think?"

"I don't think we've seen the last of these fundamentalist crazies," Mr. Ganey said, looking right at Quinn. "First *Webster*, now this. It's a slippery slope."

Quinn didn't smile at him, but she didn't turn away either.

"I sure enjoyed your class this semester," Mr. Ganey said to

Mr. Levine.

Mr. Levine laughed. "I'm glad. I did too."

As Mr. Ganey walked away, Seth reached over to squeeze Quinn's waist. He let his arm rest there. Mr. Levine's eyes went back and forth between them.

"You two have had a meeting of the minds, I see." He looked genuinely surprised.

Quinn giggled like someone had pressed the on button on a radio already set at full volume. Seth would miss that girly laugh next year. He'd miss lots of things.

Approaching Quinn's front porch the following Saturday afternoon, Seth found her dad in the front yard dividing hosta. Mr. Ganey smiled and nodded at him. He pried the spade out of the dense clump of roots at his feet and leaned the handle toward Seth.

"Hold this, will ya?" he asked, passing it to him with a dirt-caked hand.

"Sure." Seth took the spade. Mr. Ganey tried to pry apart the clump of roots with his fingers, but they were too packed. "Need help?" Seth asked, setting the tip of the spade in the middle of the clump.

"I seem to, yes. Thanks." Mr. Ganey stood and watched Seth split the clump into rough fourths with two stomps on the spade. It was like the guy expected you to be competent so you were. Seth laid the spade on the ground. Together, they knelt and pulled apart the remaining muddy roots.

Standing up, Seth gestured at the frill of white bleeding hearts growing near the porch.

"I like bleeding hearts," he said with a sly grin. He wasn't a landscaper's kid for nothing.

Mr. Ganey laughed. "Me, too." He held out his muddy hand. Seth shook it before walking up to the porch.

CHAPTER 28
CENTRAL PLANNING

"**D**o you want to?" Seth asked her. She heard his voice tremble. They'd been walking around downtown by the old train station. Quinn was leaning back against the steps of an antique steam engine. It was uncomfortable, but she felt too revved up to care. Seth hovered over her, panting, his knees straddling her hips on the middle step.

"Here?" she asked.

"Uh, I'm not sure I'm up for doing it on a train in public," he said. He pushed her hips across the step and sat next to her.

Quinn grazed the crotch of his jeans with the palm of her hand.

"It feels like you're up for anything."

"Um, yeah, but I'm a train virgin."

"Only a train virgin?" She knew he was every kind of virgin. She started to rub the front of his jeans.

"Oh, God," he moaned. "Don't do that." She stopped. "Okay, I lied. Do that." He leaned back on the steps and let her build him up to a breathless verge. Then she pushed him over it, watching his face contort and then relax. He pulled her in for a deep kiss before dropping back again on the steps.

"When though?" he asked her, still gasping.

Quinn felt ready. Seriously ready. The craving she felt now—a near-painful kind of starvation—was agonizing. And new. Her sister had been right. She checked her watch.

"I have to be home in twenty minutes." Seth waited. "Sunday?" she asked. "My parents are having brunch with friends, and I don't have to work for once. That's six days away, though."

"We don't have to, you know," Seth said, looking unconvinced.

"I want to." As she heard herself say it, a herd of butterflies stampeded up and down the sides of her stomach. "I really want to."

"So, Sunday?"

"Sunday."

CHAPTER 29
BALANCE OF POWER

S eth left the air-conditioned living room to wait for Quinn on the front porch. He needed a break from sorting books into save and giveaway piles. After packing and cleaning for weeks, the essential remains of this crumpled house would fit into his aunt's basement. Knowing this made his own essential remains feel crumpled, too.

Grief got more confusing by the day. Part of him was glad his mom was out of pain. Part of him wanted to scream at her for being such a selfish jerk. He kept her note unfolded on the dining room table to remind him of how pissed off she'd be if he wasted any more time before getting on with his "big, amazing life." But you don't bounce back right away from becoming an orphan, Seth mused. You feel like a bystander at first, like it's not even you.

It was shocking how your life kept going. The whole world should screech to a total stop; his mom had killed herself, had killed their lives together. But the streetlights still came on. The convenience store kept its regular hours. The mail turned up. The worst had gone ahead and happened, and here he was still standing, still alive.

In two weeks, he'd move to Iowa. Quinn would leave for George Washington University. Aunt Gail had ignored Seth's empty protests like he'd hoped she would; he'd spend the next few months in her crowded split-level in Des Moines while he applied to colleges for next year. If he figured out how this financial aid thing worked, he might even apply to some big-name schools. Mr. Levine had given Seth his new home address and made him promise to send regular updates on his decision-making process. It was kind of humbling that the adults in his life flatly expected him to get on with living it.

Seth sat on the front step and surveyed the neighborhood he would leave in two more weeks. The big crack in the neighbors' driveway held a respectable crop of self-sowing petunias. A shallow dip in the front lawn was all that remained of one of his mom's first projects here. A big elm tree had died and been chopped down by the city. His mom had tackled the lonely stump with an axe about the same size as she was. Seth remembered her knobby knees in her cutoff jeans. Her pink T-shirt had clung to her flat chest. She would have looked like a ten-year-old were it not for the men's leather work gloves and the unlaced steel-toed boots she wore.

Seth admired his recent, solo landscaping project. He'd spent way too much money on the four boxwood bushes, but he'd wanted to finish at least one small part of his mom's blue-sky design. He'd loosened the hard-packed topsoil and reached the fine, almost fluffy dirt underneath that she'd worked so hard to make ready for growing things. Years ago, she had dug up trenches of soil, poured in bags and bags of composted manure and handfuls of peat moss and bone meal. She'd mixed it all up with a spade as tall as she was. Neither one of them would be here to admire the new shrubs, but Seth knew they'd thrive.

Quinn pulled up to the curb in her mom's car. She waved as she got out and shut the door. She wore the short denim skirt she knew he liked. Seth watched her calves flex as she navigated the bumpy front sidewalk. He returned her flirty smile as she stopped at the bottom step in front of him. The bright morning sunlight bounced off her shiny hair.

She didn't comment on his landscaping project. Seth didn't care. He stood and held the door for her. Quinn blew past him along with a hot southern breeze.

"Nice T-shirt," she said, pulling him toward her for a kiss in the dim foyer. Her fingers squeezed the back of his neck.

"T-shirt?" He pretended to be disoriented by her iced-tea-flavored smooch. She tugged the sleeve of the Green Day shirt that Lee had bought for him at an actual *1,000 Hours* concert.

Once inside, though, Quinn's flirty smile seemed to take effort. She started to tuck and untuck her hair. Seth got a roll of duct tape off the top of the television and tossed it to her, coaxing back her real smile. As he knelt in front of a bulging cardboard box, Quinn pulled out a strip of the tape and scanned the room.

"Scissors?" she asked.

"Nope," he said. Seth braced the sides of the box, pushed the top flaps together and waited. Quinn ripped the strip of tape with her teeth. Seth liked that in a girl. As they sealed the seam between the top flaps, he grinned at her. What he meant to say was,

"I love it when you do that."

"I love you," he blurted. It felt so good to finally say the words that he said them again. "I love you."

Her eyes locked on his. "I love you, too."

On his knees, he scooted around the big box. He wrapped his arms around her soft waist, feeling her bare abdomen.

It took five seconds for their kissing to turn frantic. Seth stood and pulled her to her feet. He held her hand as they walked silently through the scrubbed kitchen and down the stairs to his room. Why hadn't he ever noticed the musty basement smell?

"Wait here," Seth told Quinn, sitting her down on the arm of his grandmother's old hide-a-bed couch. He went into his bedroom and clicked the door behind him. Now that he'd packed most of his stuff, it felt lighter in here, like the air could finally reach the corners. His hands shook as he lit six vanilla candles. He left three of them on his dresser and putting three on his bedside table. He changed his mind and moved one to the windowsill. It started to singe the closed blinds. He moved it back to the bedside table. This would not be a good time to burn down the house.

He put a Ramones tape in the boom box and pressed play. The smart-ass punk rock made him feel more hyper than romantic, although at this particular moment it was a short trip. He looked in his shoebox and found U2's *The Joshua Tree*. He tossed the other tape back into the box and pressed play on the long intro to the first song. He turned the volume down low and opened the door.

Seth stumbled on a ripple in the matted light-blue carpet as he walked back to Quinn. He took her cold hands and pulled her up to standing. He kissed her and led her into his room. She started sneezing.

"Can I blow out the candles?" she asked between sneezes. "I'm allergic."

He shook his head slowly. "Thanks a lot, buzzkill. These things cost me forty-nine cents apiece."

She laughed. He blew out the candles and smiled into her watery blue eyes until she stopped sneezing. Then he leaned down and kissed her slowly. Hopefully, this would help them both calm down. After a few minutes she pulled back from him and steadied herself against his dresser. Quinn had apparently calmed down already: she kept her eyes on his face as she unpeeled her T-shirt. What Seth wanted to do when he saw her breasts pushed together in a lacy white bra was toss her on the bed. Forcing his brain to overrule his boner, he reached out instead and touched her face. Stroking the side of her neck, he kissed the white skin between her chest and shoulder. The softness of her barely registered on his callused fingertips, but he smelled baby powder and fresh sweat. He breathed a humid path down her chest and kissed her nipple through her bra. She unclasped it and pushed it off her shoulders.

He held one of her breasts in each hand and ran his thumbs over the hard little nipples in the middle. He leaned down and took one in his mouth. She jumped so suddenly that he lost his balance. He kept himself from falling over by clutching the dresser, trapping Quinn in his flexed arms.

"Jesus!" He regained his composure slightly. He laughed a one-syllable laugh. "You scared me."

She kissed him. Her hands—warm now—pulled his palms away from the edge of the dresser and pressed them on her breasts. Ninety percent of his blood flow pulsed in his penis. It was unbearable but in the most awesome way possible. He moved his hands to thrum the sides of Quinn's ribcage with his fingers. Still kissing her, he steered her to his freshly made bed.

They sat. Seth heard his throat make a gulping noise. Awkward. Quinn nudged him to lie down. She unzipped his fly. She seemed to know what she was doing. As she started to pull down his jeans, she glanced up at him as if to ask, "Is this okay?"

Hell yes, he nodded. She tugged his jeans and gray boxers down to his thighs and crouched over him. Holy shit. Whacking off didn't even come close to this new universe of wet and warmth. At first, she moved slowly. Then she used her hands and spit and pressure to force him to the edge. As he came, Seth groaned. He ejaculated onto his abdomen; this part he knew.

Quinn flopped next to him. She propped herself up on one elbow and twirled a tuft of his light-brown chest hair. His receding orgasm left him paralyzed from the eyeballs down. She swiped Kleenex from the box on the bedside table and tentatively wiped him off. He heard her make a basket into the metal can by his desk.

"Seth?" she asked. He pressed his watering eyes into the crook of his arm. He decided to go with the urge to laugh and weep at the same time.

"Still here," he croaked. "Barely." He kicked off the jeans still bunched around his ankles and pulled his boxers back up. Kissing Quinn's neck, he rolled on top of her. He stroked one of her breasts. "Can I . . . um . . . ," he faltered. "Can I play with these for a minute?"

She laughed. He sat up and straddled her lightly so that he could give each breast equal attention. He'd touched them before, but not like this. He hefted their weight, flattened his palms and made breast pancakes. He experimented with a gentle jiggle. She watched him like he was a kitten with a new toy.

He shifted. Licking around her nipples seemed like the thing to do. It was. When he paused, she pushed up her chest to meet his mouth. He licked and stopped, licked and stopped. Quinn panted with her eyes clamped shut. He kissed a trail down her pale stomach. He unzipped and peeled down her skirt.

When he slid down her blue cotton bikini pants, she didn't open her eyes. He kissed her again where he'd left off, below her belly button and over to where her waist narrowed. Was it obvious to her that this was new territory for him? He cupped her crotch, feeling slippery wetness farther back. If he did this right, he might blow her mind. If not, she'd think he was a human cattle prod. Bono sang that he still hadn't found what he was looking for. No shit. Seth scooted down between Quinn's knees. Using a flashlight at this point would probably kill the mood. He used his thumbs to spread her folds. Her salty, baby powder smell made him hard again. He let the tip of his tongue rest for a second on what he hoped was the right spot, where the folds kind of merged together. She gasped and shivered. He did it again, getting the same reaction. Reading all those *Playboys* hadn't been for nothing.

"A little higher," she whispered. Really? He licked higher. Her gasps got louder. He wasn't a human cattle prod. "Softer," she said, stroking his hair. But he was already barely touching her. He softened his tongue and made her gasp again. He was the king of oral sex. Her breathing quickened and got shallow. She came so hard that her back lifted off the bed. Then she fell back and sort of quaked for almost a minute. Seth was impressed.

She squeezed his arm. He wiped his mouth on his pillowcase before lying down, facing her. Her body kept giving off little shivers.

"Are you cold or are you still going?" he asked her.

"Yes," she murmured.

Seth scrambled to his hands and knees. Grinning two inches from her face, he yanked down the bedspread and covers underneath her from both sides. He pretended to grunt and heave with the effort of moving her body, a pink-cheeked sack of potatoes. She laughed while he pulled the covers up over her, tucking her in feet to neck like a burrito. He flopped down next to her but on top of the bedspread. She pulled out her arms from the bedspread burrito to raise them in a long stretch.

"Aren't you cold, too?"

Horny was what he was. "Hell no." His boner wanted more attention. He wrapped a leg around her, pressing himself against her hip. "Do you still want to try this?" he asked. *Say yes, say yes.*

"Did you get the condoms?' she asked, switching into bossy school nurse mode.

"Yes, ma'am." She was on the Pill now, too, so they were all set.

He reached under his mattress and pulled out a long strip of lubricated Trojans. He'd tried to act cool yesterday when he stopped to get them at the Super C. He'd even paid for them.

"Kind of optimistic, don't you think?" she asked as she tickled his stomach.

"Just hopeful." He tore off a condom and ripped open the package. They were slippery little suckers. He tossed it to Quinn. She pulled the beige circle out of the wrapper and gestured to him to scoot over. It wouldn't unroll. Had he ever been this horny in his whole life? Seth swiped the condom from her. He turned it over and started rolling it down. She stopped him.

"Get another one. That one has goo on it."

"Goo?"

"Sperm. Spoo. Semen. You can't put it on you and then turn it the other way. It defeats the purpose." Thank God one of them still had the use of her brain. He rolled on Trojan number two, even remembering to squeeze the air out of the tip as per the health teacher with the banana.

She seemed nervous now. Seth spent a minute pretending to have lost her warm body under the layers of covers, feeling around until she laughed. He climbed under the blankets and lay on top of her while supporting most of his weight on his hands and knees.

He kissed her soft and slow. When he licked her neck, she pressed her chest against his. He loved having that kind of power, to make her body crave more. She scooted down and spread her legs a little. An inch closer and he'd be inside that wet spot.

"You sure?" he whispered, kissing her again.

She nodded and let go of a shuddery breath. "Slow, okay?"

He kissed her and moved closer, in, into slippery warmth. Pressure and texture swallowed him whole. He wanted to pound into her, chase it, but he slowed his breathing carefully.

"Should I try moving a little?"

"Mm hmm."

He tried, but even the smallest, glacial movements made it feel two seconds away. He mentally reviewed Peter Jennings's latest report on acid rain, democracy movements, blah, blah, blah. He felt himself backing away from the cliff until Quinn started tongue kissing his neck. He groaned, desperate.

"Quinn? I can't hold it anymore."

"Okay."

Yes! He moved into her two, three times and came. He buried his face in her neck as the rush peaked and ebbed out in core-shaking waves.

His arms wobbled now from supporting his weight and maybe from other stuff, too. He collapsed next to Quinn and pushed away the blankets. His penis looked ridiculous now, half-erect with a trapped blob of jizz at the end.

"So?" he asked.

She lifted his arm and bent it toward her face. She slowly kissed his wrist.

"Yum. Good. You?"

He scrunched his eyebrows. "It was okay, I guess." He pretended to stifle a yawn. Then he pushed himself up on one elbow and tickled her armpit. She thumped his chest, pushing him onto his back again. "The question now," he said, pointing at his wilting penis, "is how do I get this thing off without splattering it all over me?"

She giggled. "That's your problem."

"Thanks a lot." Seth let her bring him under the sheet. He waited for his post-O fever to break as they listened to the music. He leaned on one elbow. "I'm going to miss you, Quinn."

"Yeah, I'll bet." She pushed his chest again and grinned at him.

"No. I'm serious." He cleared his tight throat and kissed her shoulder.

Her eyes welled up fast. "Me, too. Could our timing be any worse?"

"No." He pulled her into his arms and held her there.

Ten minutes later, he staggered out of bed, trying to hold the condom on while also trying not to look like an idiot. He felt stupid walking around naked in front of Quinn. Then he felt stupid for feeling stupid in front of the girl he loved who loved him back who he'd made love to. He cupped the end of his penis, turning to smile at her as he fumbled for the doorknob. The beautiful girl in his rumpled bed put her arms behind her head and took in the full view, an appreciative audience.

CHAPTER 30
PERESTROIKA

Quinn slid past Seth in the narrow limestone passage and squeezed his butt. She was leading their own private morning tour of the Nebraska State Capitol building, which—phallic jokes aside—any fool could see was the work of a genius. First she'd made Seth stand on the lawn outside and admire the building's sunken windows and art deco vertical lines. Then she'd pointed out the gold frieze above the door.

"See there? That's the pioneers." Quinn's parents had dragged her here a dozen times over the past eighteen years. Seth shook his head and smiled at her. It wasn't until they'd reached the rotunda that he actually looked impressed. Quinn watched him admire the mosaics and check out the tribal symbols on the colorful carved doors leading to the Unicameral.

"I remember these from the tour," he said. "They're kind of cool."

She widened her eyes in a silent duh.

Now they stood on the north-facing rim of the Capitol's observation deck. Quinn tried to memorize the familiar broad sky and cotton ball clouds. Most of Nebraska was flat farmland, but from here, practically all you could see were mature trees.

The day felt sticky already. For two weeks, the temperature had climbed to ninety degrees before noon. People's lawns turned brown and shrank back into those painfully hard cones of dirt posing as grass. It wouldn't be until late September before the heat eased up and you'd start to believe that your life wouldn't end in an Easy-Bake Oven.

Seth leaned out over the observation deck's low stone wall. He took in the whole panorama before leaning back against the limestone.

"When I earn enough money for a plane ticket I'm going to come show you the real Washington, DC," he said.

Quinn nodded but her stomach clenched. Would she even know herself outside of this familiar place? Tomorrow she was leaving for college and would find out.

Months ago, she'd worried about being homesick and had plotted weekend visits to New York to visit Sarah. Lately, though, she'd wondered if she'd be homesick at all. Her parents' conversations with each other had been polite and generic for weeks. Only recently had they started thawing into warier versions of their former selves. Quinn and her dad still fumbled for things to talk about.

"Your dad loves you, you know," Seth said now, reading her mind as he pushed himself off the warm stone. He smiled. "He's a good guy."

"An arrogant one."

"Maybe. But I've met way worse. Besides, to change his mind, you'd have to change who he is."

"I tried that. It didn't work."

Seth gently pinched her arm. "Exactly." Okay, she could see his point. "I've never seen someone trust herself the way you do, like you *know*, you know? Maybe your dad gets some credit for that."

Maybe.

One time, in eighth grade, Quinn had run home from school to finish *Where the Red Fern Grows*. She'd waited all day to hunt raccoons in the Ozarks with Billy Coleman and his redbone coonhounds. An hour later, she sat bawling on the couch, undone by the tragic ending. Her dad had walked in the front door, rushed over, and sat next to her.

"Are you all right?"

Quinn had squished up her face and bawled some more, flinging a despairing gesture toward the paperback on her lap.

"Little Ann died!" She couldn't have been sadder if it had been her own dog.

Relief had washed over her dad's face, followed by the barest hint of a smile. He'd replaced it with a grave expression. "I remember reading that book to Sarah. We both cried. And I remember your mother reading *Charlotte's Web* to both of you and all three of you crying."

Quinn had nodded, wiping tears and snot on her shirt sleeve. "Still," she said, "it's kind of embarrassing to cry over a book."

"I like people who cry over books. It makes me trust them." Her dad had squeezed her leg and left her to her mourning.

Quinn smiled at the memory. She couldn't help but like people who liked people who cried over books. It made her trust them.

After driving Seth back to his house, Quinn went home to finish packing. In her room, she surveyed her open dresser drawers. She folded her jean jacket. Did freshmen on the East Coast wear sweatshirts, she wondered? Or was that like wearing a sign that said, "Hick"?

She and Ilene had had one last stack of pancakes together before Ilene had flown to Boston.

"Any regrets?" Ilene asked Quinn. "Besides dating a debater, I mean?" She smiled.

"None," Quinn said. "Honestly? I've barely thought about it. I have so much to do."

Now she heard her dad shuffling around in the slippers he'd recently patched with his beloved duct tape. On weekends, he lounged in his bathrobe, drinking coffee and listening to Beethoven or Mozart. Around noon, he'd change into his spectacularly nerdy red Nebraska Cornhuskers T-shirt. They'd been polite to each other these past few weeks, but uneasy.

He came and stood in the doorway of her room. He surveyed the sweaters and shoes heaped on her bed. His belted red flannel robe outlined his softening midsection. Quinn heard the lush strains of Debussy's "Clair de Lune" on the downstairs stereo.

"That's for you, Ace," he said, tossing a George Washington baseball cap on top of her suitcase. "It's from Mom and me."

She picked it up and admired it. "Thanks, Dad." She put it on. It felt good to be called Ace again.

"Have you packed your medical insurance forms?"

"Yes."

"Social Security card?"

"Yup."

"Okay." He frowned as he rubbed the graying stubble on his chin. He cleared his throat. "It's no fun being mad at each other, Quinn," he said, "and I'm sorry I patronized you. I was disrespectful. I apologize." She picked at the button on the cap, not knowing how to answer. He shifted to lean on the doorframe. "I think we both want the same things, though. We want our friends and families to love us, for example. We both want to feel safe. We like our privacy. We both hope to make the world a better place for everyone, not only for ourselves." Quinn nodded. "What I'm trying to say is that smart people like you and I can disagree on lots of things."

"What about you and Mom?"

"She's another smart person. She disagrees with me way more often than you know. She doesn't let me get away with much." He reached over and ruffled Quinn's hair. Then he fished in his pocket for a crumpled handkerchief. Seeing him there wiping his nose and standing in his bathrobe made Quinn feel taller all of a sudden. But she also felt unsteady, like she'd gotten a plaster cast off her leg. She put on the cap.

"So you're going to miss me, Dad?" She'd meant to sound funny, joking, but it came out wistful.

He didn't smile back and was blinking fast. "When you raise a nice girl, you like her. You want to keep her around."

Quinn spun toward her unmade bed. She rubbed away the itchy beginnings of tears as she pretended to resmooth her hair under the GW cap. She turned around again to face him. He'd composed himself now, too: he was back to regular dorky in his ratty bathrobe. She gestured to the pile of clothes on her bed.

"Wanna help me pack?"

Her dad ran a hand through his own silvering hair and shook his head with a grin that made his eyes crinkle. "Not even a little bit," he said. He stepped over a pile of clothes and hugged her before heading downstairs to his cold coffee and Debussy.

An hour later, Quinn thumped down the carpeted stairs, jumping over the creaky lowest step. As she scrounged for dry-roasted peanuts in the kitchen, she heard Van Morrison's "Brown Eyed Girl" playing at high volume in the living room. At the bridge of the song, she crept along the only two floorboards that didn't squeak. She flattened herself against the hallway wall to peep into the living room from the doorway.

Furniture that usually circled the hearth sat pressed against the walls, rumpling the large rug. Her mom's high-heeled sandals hung by their back straps from two of the Christmas-stocking hooks drilled into the mantle. She laughed and wiggled her pretty hips as she twirled. Quinn's dad, still in his bathrobe, squeezed his eyes shut and banged his head in the air to the twanging bass beat.

Quinn watched for a minute before turning and taking the stairs two at a time. She giggled to herself, shaking her head at the tragically uncool sight of an executive shaking her booty and a semi-old guy playing his heart out on an unironic air guitar.

EPILOGUE

November 16, 1989

Dear Seth,

I'm sitting in the library with my roommates, pretending to study for midterms. The science one is tomorrow. The teaching assistant needs us to know that she's bored and smarter than we are. She calls the class "Physics for Poets."

No way are you already done with your college applications! I know U of Iowa wants you bad, but I still have my fingers crossed for UVA. Mr. Levine and Aunt Gail must be proud of you. So am I.

Did East Germany's leader honestly say, "Hey everyone, go ahead and cross the border?" I can't stop watching the media coverage. I sat in my dorm room most of the day on Thursday watching all of those East and West Berliners crowding around the wall. I wanted to be there with you, drinking champagne and chanting, "Tor auf! Open the gate!"

I bawled like a baby when the people started flood-

ing through the checkpoints. Seeing two million East Berliners visiting West Berlin after being separated for forty-four years made our own separation—I admit—seem somewhat less harsh.

One reporter called it "the greatest street party in the history of the world." I know you must be watching it, too. Did you get goose bumps, watching those people ("wall woodpeckers") hammer at the wall while the bull-dozers pulled it down? I cut out a photo from the news-paper of one of the sections. Someone had spray painted on it: "Only today is the war really over."

My friends tell me they've called an emergency meet-ing, one that has to do with getting coffee. It's a little like living with my sister again. (She says hi, by the way. We're meeting in NYC next weekend.)

Love,

Quinn

GLOSSARY

AIDS—Acquired Immune Deficiency Syndrome is an immune system disease that makes a person prone to infections, certain cancers, and neurological disorders. It is caused by a retrovirus (Human Immunodeficiency Virus or HIV) and spreads to others through blood or blood products, sexual contact, or contaminated hypodermic needles. When AIDS became an epidemic in the 1980s, it was misunderstood, feared, and fatal. With the development of antiretroviral drugs, however, AIDS deaths began to decline in developed countries in 1997. It is still one of the leading causes of death worldwide: an estimated 35 million people have HIV/AIDS. Many lack access to affordable treatment.

Apartheid—the Afrikaans name given in 1948 to South Africa's institutionalized system of racial segregation. Years of violent, internal black protest, international sanctions, the country's economic struggles, and the end of the Cold War finally brought down white minority rule in the early 1990s. U.S. policy toward the white regime evolved from "look the other way" to total divestment, playing an important role in apartheid's initial survival and eventual downfall. The Cold War defined all American foreign policies; the fact that South Africa's Nationalist Party was noncommunist made it an automatic American ally despite its brutality to the black majority.

Balance of Power—the idea that international relationships can stabilize if each side is equally powerful. East and West feared that "unbalancing" actions would trigger greater conflicts or even nuclear war. The Cold War proved, however, that this bipolarity led both sides to forge questionable alliances, itself a destabilizing practice.

Berlin Wall—a fortified cement wall constructed around the Western zones of Berlin in 1961 to prevent the escape and defection of East Germans to the West. It remained a symbol and fact of Cold War division until 1989.

Central Planning—an economic system (such as the former Soviet Union's) in which economic decisions are made by the government rather than by the interaction between consumers and businesses.

Communism—a political ideology and system that strives for a society with no classes or structures of government.

Containment—President Truman's foreign policy doctrine that the Soviet Union must be "contained" within the Eastern Bloc to prevent the further spread of communism. Containment became the most important tenet of American foreign policy until the Reagan administration. It justified a quadrupling of U.S. defense spending, wars in Korea and Vietnam, the Bay of Pigs invasion, and the Cuban missile crisis.

Contras—U.S.-backed counter-revolutionaries who opposed Nicaragua's elected socialst Sandinista government (in power from 1979 to 1990).

Conventional Warfare—waging war in the open and using conventional weapons (such as guns) instead of using chemical, biological, or nuclear weapons.

Covert Intelligence—collecting information in secret and concealing the identity of the person(s) conducting the activity. Also known as spying.

Détente—a state of improved relations after a period of conflict or tension. President Nixon adopted a policy of détente in 1972, calling for a more relaxed approach to the Soviet Union. During this time, the United States and U.S.S.R. signed the Strategic Arms Limitation Talks (or SALT) treaty and the Helsinki Accords (a nonbinding East/West peace treaty). President Reagan abandoned détente (and containment) in 1980 in favor of an aggressive "rollback" policy.

Disarmament—the reduction or withdrawal of military forces and weapons.

Divestment—the corporate version of a consumer boycott: businesses take away their financial support from other businesses to promote a certain behavior or policy. Divestment in South Africa started as a grassroots movement in Sweden (a neutral party in the Cold War) in the 1960s. It took hold internationally in the mid-1980s. After the U.S. passed a law in 1986, American corporations sold their stocks in companies that did business in South Africa. American divestment had little impact on the companies themselves, but it raised awareness and the public's moral standards. It pressured whites to negotiate with blacks and, ultimately, end the apartheid regime.

Domino Theory—the commonly held belief among Cold War policy thinkers that if one country fell to communism others would follow. In 1965, the domino theory was President Johnson's main rationale in for the massive escalation of the conflict in Vietnam.

Eisenhower Doctrine—President Eisenhower pledged in 1957 to provide military and economic aid to any Middle Eastern country fighting communism.

Escalation—the process by which conflicts grow in severity over time. The term came into common usage during—and in reference to—the Cold War.

Evil Empire—the term used by President Reagan in 1983 to describe the Soviet bloc.

Fallout—the radioactive particles stirred up by or resulting from a nuclear explosion. The term also refers to a secondary and often lingering effect, result, or set of consequences.

Freedom of Access to Clinic Entrances (FACE) Act—a law signed by President Clinton in 1994. FACE bans the use or threats of force or obstruction to block a person's entry into a health clinic or place of worship. It protects abortion protesters' free speech (holding signs, distributing literature, singing hymns) while preventing them infringing on women's Fourteenth Amendment right to privacy. Under the FACE Act, abortion protesters who handcuff themselves to clinic doors or stalk abortion providers at their places of worship (common tactics employed by national anti-abortion group Operation Rescue in the 1980s) may be prosecuted for trespassing.

First-Strike Capability—the ability of one nation to launch a surprise attack on another, giving them a significant advantage. The United States enjoyed first-strike capability over the Soviet Union until the late 1950s when the Soviet Union developed the capacity to detect a theoretical first-strike. This capacity gave it second-strike capability: the power to launch its own weapons before American bombs hit their targets.

Fundamentalism—a religious belief and practice (most commonly found today in Islam and Protestant Christianity) characterized by a strict, literal interpretation of religious scripture. In the United States, fundamentalism ebbs and flows in reaction to the perceived evils of modern life and modern theological interpretation. Adherents claim religious purity, seek a return to a previous ideal, and use fear as a central tactic and weapon in a perceived battle of good versus evil. While the First Amendment protects the practice of any religion, fundamentalism has historically had a stifling effect on the public discourse on which American democracy hinges.

Glasnost—Russian for *openness*. The term refers to Soviet reforms implemented by President Gorbachev during the late 1980s that encouraged open debate, discussion, and freedom of speech.

Green Day—is an American punk rock band formed in Berkley, CA, in 1986. In 1989, it recorded its debut *1,000 Hours* album. The band helped popularize and revive mainstream American interest in punk rock. Sadly, Green Day did not perform in Lincoln, Nebraska in 1989. Their first tour outside of California was in 1990. It included eight small venues in the Midwest but none were in Nebraska.

Griswold v. Connecticut—this 1965 Supreme Court decision overturned a Connecticut ban on birth control. The court found that the ban violated the Constitution's implied "right to marital privacy," citing other constitutional protections from governmental intrusion, such as the self-incrimination clause of the Fifth Amendment. The 1973 *Roe v. Wade* decision builds on *Griswold*, making abortion legal on the same right-to-privacy grounds. *Roe's* basis in *Griswold* explains why the national antiabortion movement has never tried to repeal *Roe* directly: an attack on *Roe* equals an attack on *Griswold*. As 98% of Americans use birth control during their lifetimes, a conservative attack on the Constitution's implied right to privacy would result in political suicide.

Iron Curtain—a term invented by Winston Churchill to describe the political and physical barriers created by the Soviet Union to block itself and its satellite states from contact with Western Europe.

Living Will—this is a legal document (also known as an advance directive) in which a patient can state his or her wishes regarding life-prolonging medical treatments. Living will legislation was first introduced in California in 1974. By 1992, all fifty states, as well as the District of Columbia, had passed legislation to legalize some form of advance directive. In 1989, however, living wills were still illegal in Nebraska.

Marshall Plan—a U.S.-financed ten-billion-dollar relief package devised by President Truman and Secretary of State George Marshall that committed to rebuilding sixteen Western and Southern European nations after World War II. The Marshall Plan was highly successful in restabilizing the area politically and economically. It is an example of how effective "soft diplomacy" can be when backed by Americans' political will.

Mujahideen—Islamic resistance fighters who battled against the Soviet Union—with American weapons and support—during its 1979–1989 occupation of Afghanistan. The term means "soldier of God" in Arabic.

Multiple Sclerosis (MS)—a disease in which an abnormal response of the body's immune system attacks the central nervous system (the brain, spinal cord, and optic nerves).

Mutually Assured Destruction (MAD)—the Cold War assumption that both the U.S. and U.S.S.R. would not launch nuclear weapons because each knew the other would retaliate, leading to devastation on both sides.

Perestroika—Russian for *restructuring*, this refers to a 1980s reform movement in the Soviet Union led by Mikhail Gorbachev. It moved the country away from state control, allowed multiple candidates to run for the same office, and legalized private ownership of businesses. It also led to a food shortage. But scholars credit perestroika as a vehicle for Soviet citizens to criticize their country publicly for the first time in forty years—in and of itself a restructuring.

Political Correctness—the avoidance of forms of expression or action that are perceived to exclude, marginalize, or insult groups of people who are socially disadvantaged or suffer discrimination. Mainstream usage of the term began in the late 1980s by conservative politicians to convey their concerns about free speech and liberals' influence in academia and culture.

Proxy War—a conflict in which larger nations support smaller nations that are involved in a war or civil war, without becoming directly involved themselves.

Radioactive—the state of giving off of rays of energy or particles by the breaking apart of atoms of certain elements (as uranium). The fallout from a nuclear bomb is radioactive: as particles decay, the energy released into the environment can kill human cells and cause cancerous mutations to DNA.

Red Dawn—a 1984 film set during World War III in Midwestern America. A group of teenagers band together to defend their town, and their country, from invading Soviet forces.

Roe v. Wade—a 1973 Supreme Court ruling that a woman's

right to have an abortion is constitutionally protected by the Fourteenth Amendment's implied right to privacy (first recognized in *Griswold v. Connecticut*). The decision legalized abortion at every stage of pregnancy. But it also defined the ways in which states could regulate abortion in the second and third trimesters, provided that those regulations did not impose an "undue burden" on the woman. The ruling affected laws in forty-six states. Ironically, the organized "pro-life" movement did not emerge until after *Roe*, the point at which American women stopped dying for the privilege of aborting an unwanted pregnancy.

Rollback—a policy advocated by President Reagan, who wanted to reduce the size of the Soviet bloc, rather than contain it or engage with it in a working relationship.

Second-Strike Capability—having the power to perceive and respond to an attack before enemy bombs hit their targets.

Strategic Defense Initiative (SDI) or **Star Wars**—President Reagan's missile defense system project, initiated in 1983. It included early warning systems, missile interception systems, and research into the use of armed satellites to protect the U.S. from Soviet ballistic missiles. Sporadic investments in missile defense started in 1962, but SDI remains the most concerted and expensive effort of the past sixty years. Between 1962 and 1996, the United States spent nearly one hundred billion dollars on missile defense programs. We do not yet have an effective ballistic missile shield.

Tiananmen Square—a large public plaza in Beijing, China, in which Mao Zedong proclaimed a communist victory in October 1949 and Chinese troops crushed a student democracy demonstration in June 1989.

Truman Doctrine—in 1947, President Truman pledged American support for all "free peoples" fighting communist aggression from foreign or domestic sources. He convinced Congress to grant four hundred million dollars to Greece and Turkey to help fight pro-Soviet insurgents. Besides committing the United States to the policy of containment, the language of the Truman Doctrine helped characterize the Cold War as a conflict between good and evil.

The Day After—a 1983 American television film watched by more than 100 million people during its first broadcast. It tells the story of a fictional war between American and Soviet allies that escalates into nuclear war.

U.S.S.R.—the Union of Soviet Socialist Republics encompassed fifteen nations: Russia, Ukraine, Georgia, Belarus, Uzbekistan, Armenia, Azerbaijan, Kazakhstan, Kyrgyzstan, Moldova, Turkmenistan, Tajikistan, Latvia, Lithuania, and Estonia.

Vietnam War—a Southeast Asian conflict (1955–1975) between communist North Vietnam's Viet Cong (backed by China and the Soviet Union) and noncommunist South Vietnam (actively supported by the United States from 1965 to 1975). It ended with the 1975 takeover of Vietnam by communist forces. Over two million people are reported to have died in Vietnam, Laos, and Cambodia, half of them civilians. Over 130,000 South Vietnamese resettled in the United States. In 1975, Cambodia and Laos also fell to communist forces, creating a steady flow of refugees from all three countries to the U.S. from 1975 to 1990.

Webster v. Reproductive Health Services—in a 5–4 decision in 1989, the Supreme Court upheld a Missouri statute that said that human life began at conception. It also barred the use of public funds for abortion, prohibited abortions at public health facilities, and required physicians to test for fetal viability after the ninteenth week of pregnancy. This decision marked the first time in twenty-six years that the court failed to affirm the *Roe v. Wade* decision that made abortion legal in 1973.

World War III—hypothetically, the next worldwide conflict. The most common Cold War scenario—an imagined nuclear war between the U.S. and the U.S.S.R.—was widely alluded to in books, films, television productions, and video games.

Zones of Occupation—after World War II, the Allies divided Germany into U.S., French, British, and Soviet zones of occupation. In 1949, the three western zones were reconstituted as West Germany; the Soviet zone became East Germany. West Germany reunified with East Germany in 1990.

Do you have a suggestion to add to this list? Please contact the author through her website at **www.katiepierson.net**.

1989 TIMELINE

January 20—George Herbert Walker Bush is inaugurated as forty-first U.S. president.

February 2—The last Soviet Union troops leave Kabul, ending a nine-year military occupation of Afghanistan.

February 3—A military coup overthrows Alfredo Stroessner, dictator of Paraguay since 1954.

February 10—President Bush and Canada's prime minister, Brian Mulroney, meet in Ottawa and lay the groundwork for the Acid Rain Treaty of 1991.

February 14—Iran's Ayatollah Khomeini bans Indian-born British author Salman Rushdie's book *The Satanic Verses* and issues a *fatwa* calling for his death.

February 14—The United States places the first of twenty-four Global Positioning System (GPS) satellites into orbit.

March 3—Portugal wins the FIFA World Cup tournament, defeating Nigeria 2–0 in Riyadh, Saudi Arabia.

March 11—A South African law commission publishes a working paper calling for the abolition of apartheid.

March 13—Tim Berners-Lee writes a proposal that will become the blueprint for the World Wide Web.

March 15—Israel hands over Taba to Egypt, ending a seven-year territorial dispute.

March 23—Serbia revokes the autonomy of Kosovo—a province with an Albanian majority—triggering six days of rioting during which twenty-nine people die.

March 24—The U.S. Congress approves forty-one million dollars in aid for Nicaragua's Contra rebels.

March 24—*Exxon Valdez*, an oil tanker, runs aground in Prince William Sound, Alaska, spilling an estimated 240,000 barrels (eleven million gallons) of oil and polluting over three thousand miles of shoreline.

March 29—*Rain Man* wins the Oscar for best picture at the Academy Awards. Dustin Hoffman wins best actor for *Rain Man*, and Jodie Foster wins best actress for *The Accused*. Geena Davis wins best supporting actress for *The Accidental Tourist*, and Kevin Kline wins best supporting actor for *A Fish Called Wanda*.

April 1—Cuba begins its twenty-seven-month withdrawal from Angola as per the recently signed Three Powers Accord, which also calls for the withdrawal of South African troops from Angola and Namibia, and the independence of Namibia.

April 3—A Food and Drug Administration advisory committee recommends approval of Norplant, a long-acting contraceptive implant that protects a woman from pregnancy for up to five years.

April 8—Madonna releases her hit single "Like a Prayer." She loses her Pepsi sponsorship when religious groups complain that the video is blasphemous.

April 9—Over three hundred thousand pro-choice activists march on Washington to protest pending cases before the Supreme Court that could potentially reverse 1973's *Roe v. Wade.*

April 14—The U.S. government seizes the Lincoln Savings and Loan Association. The massive 1980s savings and loan crisis costs U.S. taxpayers nearly two hundred billion dollars in bailouts and many people their life savings.

April 17—Tens of thousands of Chinese students take over Beijing's Tiananmen Square to demand increased democracy in China.

April 23—Iraqi President Saddam Hussein's two-year genocide campaign against the Kurdish minority ends. It consisted of two years of summary executions, mass disappearances, the widespread use of chemical weapons, and the destruction of over two thousand villages.

April 25—Motorola introduces the MicroTAC Personal Cellular Telephone, the world's smallest mobile phone.

April 26—The Daulatpur-Saturia tornado, the deadliest ever recorded, kills thirteen hundred people in Bangladesh.

May 4—A U.S. jury convicts Oliver North for his involvement in the Iran-Contra affair. He claimed to have acted on orders when he arranged arms deals with Iran and diverted the profits to Nicaraguan Contras. He admitted to lying to Congress in order to cover up his role in the scandal.

May 10—Panamanian military dictator Manuel Noriega denies the electoral victory of his opponent Guillermo Endara and sponsors violent attacks on him and his supporters. Seven months later, the United States invades Panama and swears in Endara as the new president.

May 17—More than one million Chinese protesters join the original group of university students in marching through Beijing, demanding greater democracy.

May 19—In the season finale of the television drama *Dallas*, Sue Ellen reveals her plan to make a tell-all movie on J.R. Ewing and make him "the laughingstock of Texas."

May 25—Mikhail Gorbachev becomes president of the Soviet Union.

June 3—Authorized by Chinese president Deng Xiaoping, government tanks kill two thousand prodemocracy protesters in Tiananmen Square. Witnesses share the news with the outside world via fax machines.

June 4—Solidarity, Poland's prodemocracy party, sweeps to victory in Poland's first free election in forty years. This was the first of many anticommunist revolutions in Central and Eastern Europe in 1989.

June 12—The Corcoran Gallery of Art removes Robert Mapplethorpe's gay photography exhibition. A controversial national debate ensues about whether tax dollars should support the arts and whether revoking federal funding infringes on artists' First Amendment rights.

June 21—The Supreme Court rules that the Constitution's guarantee of free speech includes the act of trampling or burning the national flag.

July 1—A study by the National Gay and Lesbian Task force reports 7,248 incidents of violence against gays during the previous year.

July 3—The *Webster v. Reproductive Health Services* Supreme Court decision upholds a Missouri statute stating that human life begins at conception. It also bars the use of public funds for abortion, prohibits abortions at public health facilities, and requires physicians to test for fetal viability after the nineteenth week of pregnancy. This decision marks the first time in twenty-six years that the court failed to affirm the *Roe v. Wade* decision that made abortion legal in the United States in 1973.

July 5—President Botha of South Africa meets the imprisoned Nelson Mandela for the first time.

July 5—The television show *Seinfeld* premieres.

July 6—The first Palestinian suicide attack on Israel takes place on Tel Aviv/Jerusalem bus number 405.

July 9—Steffi Graf and Boris Becker of West Germany win singles tennis titles at Wimbledon.

July 20—Military police place Burmese democracy leader Aung San Suu Kyi under house arrest. She is freed twenty-one years later in 2010.

July 31—Nintendo releases the Game Boy portable video game system in North America.

July 31—The presidents of five Central American countries agree that the U.S.-backed Contras fighting Nicaragua's government should be disbanded and evicted from their bases in Honduras.

August 9—Army General Colin R. Powell is appointed as the first black chairman of the Joint Chiefs of Staff.

August 23—Two million indigenous people of Estonia, Latvia, and Lithuania join hands to demand freedom and independence from Soviet occupation, forming an uninterrupted six-hundred-kilometer human chain called the Baltic Way.

September 17–22—Hurricane Hugo devastates the Caribbean and the southeastern United States, causing at least seventy-one deaths and eight billion dollars in damage.

September 22—An Irish Republican Army bomb explodes at the Royal Marine School of Music in Deal, Kent, United Kingdom, leaving eleven dead and twenty-two injured.

September 23—A cease-fire in the Lebanese Civil War stops the violence that has claimed nine hundred lives since March.

September 26—Vietnam withdraws its last troops from Cambodia, ending an eleven-year occupation.

October 1—Civil unions between same-sex partners become legal in Denmark, the world's first such legislation.

October 13—The Dow Jones Industrial Average plunges 190.58 points (6.91%) after the junk bond market collapses.

October 21—President George Bush vetoes a bill approved by Congress that would allow Medicaid funds to pay for abortions for low-income women who were victims of "promptly reported" rape or incest.

November 9—Thousands of jubilant Germans tear down the Berlin Wall. Just as the Wall had come to represent the division of Europe, its fall came to represent the end of the Cold War.

November 12—Brazil holds its first free presidential election since 1960, marking the first time that all Ibero-American nations, excepting Cuba, had elected constitutional governments simultaneously.

November 17—Riot police violently beat back a peaceful student demonstration in Prague, Czechoslovakia. Over the next few days, the number of protesters swells from two hundred thousand to an estimated half million. The Velvet Revolution against the communist government succeeds on December 29.

November 17—Disney's *The Little Mermaid* opens in theaters.

December 3—Weeks after the fall of the Berlin Wall, U.S. president George H. W. Bush and Soviet leader Mikhail Gorbachev release statements from their conference near Malta. They call for further cuts in conventional and nuclear weapons. This signals to the world their shared belief that the Cold War is ending.

December 6—British television broadcasts the last episode of the classic era of *Doctor Who*.

December 9—The United States crushes a military coup attempt against the government of Philippine President Corazon Aquino.

December 19—Romanian workers strike in protest of the country's brutal communist regime. A week later, the army joins the popular uprising and executes President Ceaușescu and his wife.

December 20—The United States invades Panama (Operation Just Cause) and imprisons dictator Manuel Noriega.

December 24—the Dalai Lama wins the Nobel Peace Prize.

December 31—Statistics show that 27,408 Americans died of AIDS in 1989, an increase of over 7,000 from the previous year.

What did you think of '89 Walls? Post your review on your favorite retailer's website through **www.katiepierson.net**.

FURTHER READING

1980s

Aristotle and Dante Discover the Secrets of the Universe by Benjamin Alire Saenz

Bitter Melon by Cara Chow

Children of the River by Linda Crew

Eleanor & Park by Rainbow Rowell

Gringolandia by Lyn Miller-Lachmann

Paper Covers Rock by Jenny Hubbard

Out of Shadows by Jason Wallace

The Scar Boys by Len Vlahos

White Lines by Jennifer Banash

Citizen Action

First Boy by Gary Schmidt

The Gospel According to Larry by Janet Tashjian

Hope Was Here by Joan Bauer

Memory Boy by Will Weaver

The President's Daughter by Ellen Emerson White

Quaking by Kathryn Erskine

Seeing Red by Kathryn Erskine

Soccer Chick Rules by Dawn Fitzgerald

Two Boys Kissing by David Levithan

The Vigilante Poets of Selwyn Academy by Kate Hattemer

Wide Awake by David Levithan

Cold War

The Boy on the Bridge by Natalie Standiford

Catch a Tiger by the Toe by Ellen Levine

Come in from the Cold by Marsha Qualey

Countdown by Deborah Wiles

Fallen Angels by Walter Dean Myers

Fallout by Todd Strasser

For What It's Worth by Janet Tashjian

Going Over by Beth Kephart

Life: An Exploded Diagram by Mal Peet

Sekret by Lindsay Smith

Positive Sexuality

Dramarama by E. Lockhart

Forever by Judy Blume

Grasshopper Jungle by Andrew Smith

Jellicoe Road by Melina Marchetta

Keeping You a Secret by Julie Anne Peters

Looking for Alaska by John Green

Lost It by Kristen Tracy

The Miseducation of Cameron Post by Emily M. Danforth

Nick and Norah's Infinite Playlist by Rachel Cohn and David Levithan

Openly Straight by Bill Konigsberg

Sex & Violence by Carrie Mesrobian

Where the Stars Still Shine by Trish Doller

Wildlife by Fiona Wood

Teen Pregnancy and Abortion

And We Stay by Jenny Hubbard

Every Little Thing in the World by Nina de Gramont

Gabi, a Girl in Pieces by Isabel Quintero

Gingerbread by Rachel Cohn

I Know It's Over by C. K. Kelly Martin

In Trouble by Ellen Levine

It's Not What You Expect by Norma Klein

Love & Haight by Susan Carlton

My Darling, My Hamburger by Paul Zindel

My Life as a Rhombus by Varian Johnson

November Blues by Sharon M. Draper

Staying Fat for Sarah Byrnes by Chris Crutcher

Do you have a suggestion to add to this list? Please contact the author through her website at **www.katiepierson.net**.

BIBLIOGRAPHY

African National Congress. http://www.anc.org.za/.

Alpha History. "The Cold War." http://alphahistory.com/coldwar/.

Avert. "AIDS Timeline." http://www.avert.org/aids-timeline.htm.

Best Teachers' Pages/Library Projects. "CNN's Cold War Glossary." http://www.bestlibrary.org/best_teachers/2008/05/cold-war-glossa. html/.

Brzezinski, Zbigniew. *Second Chance: Three Presidents and the Crisis of American Superpower.* New York: Basic Books, 2007.

Central Intelligence Agency. "World Fact Book: South Africa." https:// www.cia.gov/library/publications/the-world-factbook/geos/sf.html.

Corona, Laurel. *South Africa.* San Diego: Lucent Books, 2000.

Crocker, Chester. "Southern Africa: Eight Years Later." *Foreign Affairs Journal.* 1989;68(4):144–164.

Dovere, Edward-Isaac. "Missile Defense Debate Reignites." *Politico.* April 13, 2012. http://www.politico.com/news/stories/0412/75090. html.

Downing, David. *Apartheid in South Africa.* Chicago: Heinemann, 2004.

Elliott, Michael. "*Time's* Annual Journey: 1989." *Time.* June 18, 2009. http://content.time.com/time/specials/packages/article/0,28804,1902809_1902810_1905185,00.html.

Encyclopedia of the New American Nation. http://www.AmericanForeignRelations.com/.

Feminist Majority Foundation. http://www.feminist.org/.

Friedman, Thomas. "U.S. Seeks Policy on South Africa." *New York*

Times. June 28, 1989. http://www.nytimes.com/1989/06/28/world/us-seeks-policy-on-south-africa.html.

Green Day Official Website. http://www.greenday.com/.Guttmacher Institute. "Legal Birth Control Turns 40." http://www.guttmacher.org/media/inthenews/2005/06/06/index.html.

Harvard University Institute of Politics. http://www.iop.harvard.edu/.

Hillegass, Linda L. *Flower Gardening in the Hot Midwest: USDA Zone 5 and Lower Zone 4.* Urbana: University of Illinois Press, 2000.

Infoplease, Pearson Education. "News and Events of 1989." http://www.infoplease.com/year/1989.html.

Mairs, Nancy. "On Being a Cripple." *Plaintext: Essays.* Tucson: University of Arizona Press, 1986.

Marty, Myron A. *Daily Life in the United States, 1960–1990: Decades of Discord.* Westport: Greenwood Press, 1997.

NARAL Pro-Choice America. http://www.naral.org/.

National Multiple Sclerosis Society. http://www.nationalmssociety.org/.

Nelan, Bruce W. "Changes in South Africa." *Foreign Affairs Journal.* 1990;69(1):135–151.

Office of the Historian, Bureau of Public Affairs, United States Department of State. "Milestones." https://history.state.gov/milestones.*POV,* PBS. "Glossary of Cold War Terms." http://www.pbs.org/pov/myperestroika/glossary.php.

Schwartz, Stephen I. "The Real Price of Ballistic Missile Defenses." WMD Junction. April 13, 2012. http://wmdjunction.com/120413_missile_defense_costs.htm.

The New York Times Company. "The AIDS Epidemic: 1988–1990." http://partners.nytimes.com/library/national/science/aids/timeline88-90.html.

White, John K. "What to Do? The Democratic Party in the 1980s." *Polity.* 1989;21(3):612–629.

Wikipedia. "1989." http://en.wikipedia.org/wiki/1989.Wikipedia. "Green Day." http://en.wikipedia.org/wiki/Green_Day.

Williams, Neville, ed. *Chronology of World History: Vol. IV: 1901–1908: The Modern World.* Oxford: Helicon Publishing, 1999.

ACKNOWLEDGMENTS

Linda Nelson, my seventh-grade English teacher at Irving Junior High, made me write. My twelfth-grade social studies teacher at Lincoln High School, Jim Barstow, made me think.

Goodenough College—our academic fraternity in London, England—offered intellectual refuge, international friendships, and precious time, despite our lowly status as Americans abroad during the final year of the Bush administration.

The librarians at the Ridgedale Public Library and the women in my Ridgedale YMCA dance class continue to be my unsuspecting colleagues.

Smart people who know stuff helped me research politics, culture, history, and horticulture. They are Melissa Akin, Juli Andersen, Elisabeth Aune, Jill Baker, Jim Bernard, Adam T. "Buck" Branting, Nicole Cockburn, Steve Cwodzinski, Joshua Dow, Lonnie Pierson Dunbier (thanks, Mom!), Deb Evnen, Robert Frame, Andrea Galdames, Carolyn Goodwin, Dick Herman, Jim Hewitt, Linda Hillegass, Karen Janovy, Virginia "Cuz" Johnson, Stephen Lay, Jochen Mankart, Jim McKee, Matthew McNeil, Katherine Meerse, Suzanne Merideth, Virginia "VJ" Nelson,

John Pierson, Mavis Pierson, Ylva Rodny-Gumede, Kay Siebler, Hussein Samatar, Marco Spinar, Laura Sweet, Robbie Weisel, and David Woodard. Special thanks to my Facebook pals who stepped up en masse to supply pop culture and geographic details.

Supportive friends, Loft Literary Center instructors, and fellow writers critiqued manuscript drafts, encouraged me, and/or told me to buck up at key stages: Beth Ain, Bev Austin, Gail Bakkom, Lonnie Pierson Dunbier, Julie Enersen, Cheryl Family, Andrea Foroughi, Robert Frame, Linda Hillegass, Jean Holt, JJ Kahle, Nancy Johnsen, Sue Johnson, Ben Jones, Kathleen "George" Kearney, Judy Kerr, Midge Kolderie, Kate Lofton, Tara Lukas, Rob MacEntarffer, Elizabeth Mosier, Elizabeth Neid, Emma Pottenger, Javier Reyes, Katherine Meerse, Mary Carroll Moore, Laura Bradley Rede, Marion Rosenbaum, Anne Tews Schwab, Emily Scribner-O'Pray, Mara Shapiro, Glynis Shea, Diane Smason, Nissa Sturgeon, Faith Sullivan, Laura Sweet, Emily Gray Tedrowe, Natalie Tower, Robbie Weisel, and Sue Wharfe.

Professional editors told me the painful truth—in detail—but with the utmost compassion. Thank you, Deborah Halvorson, Laura Petrella, Ashley Shelby, and Craig Taylor. Patrick Maloney, Wise Ink intern, bravely took on '89 Walls as his first proofreading project. Carrie Mesrobian suggested in the kindest possible way that I put on my big-girl pants already and do a massive revision. She rules.

I received generous professional advice on marketing and the mysterious workings of the publishing industry from Jim Bernard, Vickie Bijur, Loel Brooks, Amy Brugh, Roseanne Cheng, Chris Crutcher, Nina de Gramont, Kathryn Erskine, Amy Gash,

John Janovy Jr., Andrew Karre, Ted Kolderie, Katherine Meerse, Julie Schumacher, Ashley Shelby, Jordan Sonnenblick, Doug Stewart, Saba Sulaiman, Anne Ursu, and Will Weaver

I'm grateful to Dara Beevas, my publishing partner and project manager at Wise Ink, for helping me produce a book that meets our respective, insanely exacting standards—and for making it a pleasure. No writers were harmed in the publication of this novel.

My daughters, Bryn and Paige, approach adulthood with such humbling wisdom, kindness, and humor that I strive to do better—and be better—in order to deserve them. They cheerfully board the next roller coaster and make the whole ride worth it.

In 2006, my partner, Jon Kahle, told me to trust myself with the insubstantial dream of writing a young adult novel. Then he closed my office door. He played with My Little Ponies, did laundry, taught seventh graders, took us to England for a sabbatical year, qualified us for health insurance, and earned a paycheck. That he's a rotten editor ("It's great, honey!") is one of his finer virtues. If he'd cared less or done less, this book would still be a vague idea that I sort of had that one time. I love you, Jon.

Sign up to receive a single email about my next book at
www.katiepierson.net!